FOUNDRY

FOUNDRY

ELIOT PEPER

Book design by Kevin Barrett Kane
Cover concept by Peter Nowell
Typeset in 11/16 Sabon LT Pro

Telling a story is like riding a bicycle.

To keep your balance, you must keep moving.

1

It wasn't that she was holding a gun to my head. It was that I could see the safety was still on. She thought I was completely at her mercy, which was what put her at mine.

My eyes flick away. Not to the briefcase hidden under the bed, never that. Instead, billowing curtains. Bright blue domes. Whitewashed walls. Turquoise sea.

You don't often catch a break in my line of work. And when you do, it almost always turns out to be a break as in leg rather than a break as in luck. But experience is a trap as often as it's a guide. You get too jaded, too paranoid, and suddenly defeat is the only certainty because every victory is suspect. I've had friends take that road, and let me tell you, they never came back. Self-doubt corroded them away like hydrofluoric acid dissolving an inconvenient corpse. That's not me, man. Me? I'm all about the *dance*.

That's what this is right here. That's what *everything* is, underneath. The dance. Miss a step, lose your head. Or maybe your soul. But when the band's on fire and you're feeling the rhythm and you've had just the right amount of rum and your feet are thinking for themselves? Nothing beats that. Nothing. Nations could rise and fall around you and you wouldn't even know it.

That's why I'm here right now.

That's why she's here, too, though she'd never admit it.

If I was pointing a gun at her forehead right now, that's what I'd ask her: wanna dance?

But it's the other way around, and if I want to catch this hard-to-believe-but-impossible-to-ignore break, I've gotta *sell* it.

"Was it really that bad, Caroline?" I ask. "You know I pride myself on being a generous lover."

Throttle the insouciance. She doesn't just know me, she *knows* me. Too much snark would imply I'm not taking this seriously. On the other hand, I'm not the kind of guy who'd be reduced to cowering by the surprise intercession of a postcoital armed interrogation, so blubbering would be a dead giveaway. Possibly, literally. No. I need just the right amount of cortisol-laced stoicism. I need to look like a guy trying to stay cool in a deeply unpleasant situation instead of a guy *pretending* to look like a guy trying to stay cool in a deeply unpleasant situation. They say the best salespeople never have job titles with "sales" in them—which is just the kind of psychological jujitsu I need to channel right now. Make that quota. Earn that commission, baby.

"Goddamnit, Adrian," she says. "I haven't used that name in ages."

I shrug, careful not to jostle the barrel pressing into my forehead. "Risk you run living undercover. You'll always be Caroline to me. You can tug the line, but the anchor's stuck."

When you shuffle passports like playing cards, it's easy to forget that others don't shrug off your interim alias as easily as you do. To you, it was always a lie anyway. To them, it's the only true thing they thought they knew about you. Names have power, and power is rarely symmetrical. Honestly, espionage is more trouble than it's worth—unless you're an intrigue junkie like me, which, frankly, I do not recommend, and cannot escape.

She narrows her eyes. This is a worrying development. Caroline does not emote lightly. I've seen her silence a dictator-for-life with an index finger. Her glare can melt titanium. And, once, on a moonless night spent high on a wind-blasted Tibetan plateau, I glimpsed a critically endangered species, possibly extinct: the dimple from a genuine, fleeting smile that outshone the Milky Way. So you can see why my sphincter attempted to retreat into my lower intestine when those luminous black eyes cinched down to slits.

"Uhhh," I say.

Yeah, I know: eloquent. Cut me some slack, OK? I'm

sitting here half-dressed on a chaise longue facing an armed maniac. What, you think that if you put yourself in my shoes right now, you'd be able to pop off a snappy rejoinder or improvise a limerick? Well, fuck you because I didn't even have time to put on my shoes! Patinated leather boat shoes sitting right there on the carpet like an oversaturated Instagram ad targeting stress-addled Connecticut hedge-fund managers forever putting off their dreams of retiring to Martha's Vineyard. So next time you are tempted to backseat drive this particular narrative, remember that you are *way* out of your fucking depth.

This is my story and I'm sticking to it, asshole.

And that's when she pops the question.

2

No. She did not ask me to become her lawfully wedded husband.

I mean, that would have been bad, but manageably so. She has insufferable taste in music. Bill Evans. Nina Simone. Maybe a little Fela Kuti when the green tea is brewed especially strong. Whereas I listen to *real* music from the likes of Taylor Swift and Olivia Rodrigo when I'm not singing along to Celia Cruz. But maybe we could like, you know, embrace the whole suburbia scene and drink seasonal Frappuccinos and send our bratty kids to charter school and keep an off-grid insulated yurt in Kamchatka for whenever we really need to blow off some steam. Also, I can't deny we have sexual chemistry, although any chemist can tell you how fast things can get out of hand with volatile reagents.

But this was no proposal.

This was a gambit.

I love gambits. They're sorta my thing. I once bet my left thumb that I could guess the private key to a cleaver-bearing Berliner's hardware wallet on the last chance he had before the wicked thing permanently locked away his hundred and fifty million dollars' worth of Ethereum inside a Gordian knot of encryption—and I'm left-handed! I walked away with my thumb, a twenty-mil equivalent fee, and a large favor in the credit column with one of German intelligence's top code monkeys. Dude's cleaver looked *sharp*, though. Serious gleam. Better than a dull cleaver, when you get right down to it, although you gotta wonder *why* he whetstones the motherfucker so diligently.

But this gambit? I did *not* love this gambit. Not one little bit.

"You just had to go there, didn't you?"

"I'm not going anywhere," she says. "I'm Buddha chillin' under the Bodhi Tree. I'm Thoreau at Walden Pond. You're the one who has to go there."

"You know, it's not too late to pivot this whole situation into some kind of sex thing," I say. "It's definitely an aggressive flavor of kink, but I'm sure I could get into it if you give me half a chance."

"The world's most anal-retentive actuary couldn't calculate how small your chances are if he snorted a Scarface-worthy mountain of Ritalin," she says, which, I must say, is a gripping mental image. "And that's quite enough evasion. Blowhard charm won't wriggle you out of this one. Get on with it."

She twists her wrist as if she's using the end of the barrel to turn a screw through my forehead into my frontal lobe—an apt metaphor for this slippery thing between us that normal people refer to as a "relationship" without realizing that their arguments over who took out the cat litter and timid make-up sex are but pale shadows cast by the stratospheric highs and cataclysmic lows of those ill-fated few of us whose personal lives are hopelessly entangled with the ebb and flow of that greatest of games, the game that subsumes all other games, the only game that really matters: power.

Of course, a high-stakes lifestyle is more about style than life. Just drop in on any Poker King Club high-rollers when they're *not* in the middle of playing a hand of no-limit hold 'em in the back room and you'll see exactly what I mean. Spoiler alert: it's gosh-darn sad. When you care that much about chips, odds are chips will be the only thing you're left with, if you're lucky.

In fact, chips are an integral part of the long, winding, bandit-infested road that led us to this picturesque boutique hotel overlooking the wine-dark Aegean. And not just chips on shoulders, though there were more than enough of those.

"Mindanao?" I ask, having considered and rejected outright denial.

"Mindanao," she says, the last syllable thrown wide like

the lid of Pandora's box.

Well, fuck.

My only consolation is that, one way or the other, this will all be over very, very soon.

3 ═══════════════════

═══════════════ **A few thoughts on tactics.**

If you're a pro interrogating an amateur, you can get away with all sorts of sneaky shit. Has a meditation teacher ever told you to "quiet your monkey mind"? Did it make you want to punch them in their self-satisfied face? If it didn't, I don't believe you, but if you're not lying to yourself as well as me, then you're a whole lot more enlightened than yours truly. Despite my smoldering resentment, the robe-sporting, sage-burning, koan-citing motherfucker has a point: your brain isn't an intellectual sanctum. It's a flesh and blood organ. It's not a rational place. It's an animal place. If you think you're different, if you think you're some unique paragon of mental clarity and rigor, then—cue chef's kiss—you're the freshest of fresh meat. Because while your meditation teacher might be able to calm your monkey for the briefest of *om*'s, a seasoned interrogator can have your monkey doing backflips and reciting poetry and shaving its own tail within minutes. Your gray matter is clay on a pro's wheel.

Caroline, bless her vicious heart, is a pro. As such, she knows she's dealing with a pro, *moi*. And when you're a pro interrogating a pro, it's a whole different can of mindfuck.

You're probably thinking aluminum briefcases packed with neatly arranged scalpels and bone saws. But torture, while the Hollywood (and Beltway) villains of the world never seem to tire of it, gets you what you want to hear, not what you need to hear. Plus, Caroline isn't a sadist. Or, more precisely, she's a much subtler and more ingenious sadist than your average overly enthusiastic barber-surgeon.

What I'm dealing with here is all about subtext, not thumbscrews. Psychological prestidigitation. A pro of Caroline's caliber doesn't just get under your skin or into your head. She spelunks into the dark center of your beating heart and snatches your juiciest secrets like Indiana Jones. Luckily, the heart thumping in this particular chest is lined with some truly nasty boobytraps—stuff that would never be allowed in an NC-17 movie, let alone a swashbuckling PG-13 adventure flick. Careful, Indy, we're taking off the training wheels.

The way this pro-on-pro *Jeopardy* is supposed to go is

that I respect that Caroline isn't messing around and won't hesitate to blow my head off and she respects that I'm going to be the slyest bastard I can manage while maintaining my soul's tenuous connection to this here body.

So asking me about Mindanao isn't merely a question. Asking me about Mindanao is a jolt of current straight to the testicles. Because Caroline is not supposed to know about Mindanao. I mean, nobody's supposed to know about Mindanao, but she's *definitely* not supposed to know about Mindanao. Caroline is making a point. She's saying: *Why, hello there, my dear chap. Yes, as a matter of fact, I know far more than you think I know and I'll make damn sure you'll never know exactly how much more I know than you think I should know because that way you can't know whether or when or how to lie without me catching you like a Florida retiree in an email phishing scheme starring a Nigerian prince with temporary cash flow issues.*

But what Caroline doesn't know is that this is a *reverse* interrogation. Booby trap number one: the safety's still on. She might be prepared to blow my head off, but her equipment isn't. So every question she asks tells me more about what she *actually* knows. Every time she drops a truth bomb, I scurry around picking up the shrapnel and assembling it into a jigsaw puzzle of what's between her ears. Oh, the hubris of thinking you have the high ground.

So here's my play: Say everything. Reveal nothing.

You want to hear about Mindanao? Sure, fine. But watch out because I'm laying a trail of tasty fucking breadcrumbs to tease out your next best question until all your clever interrogatives snap into place and I know *you*, motherfucker, I *know* you.

Thing is, you can't make sense of Mindanao without understanding Miami.

4

Miami, bitch-queen of cities.

Miami, with its canals to channel the rising sea, laissez-faire social norms, pastel highlights, unlikely but endearing appreciation for the profoundly weird, and humidity that turns the air to Jell-O.

Miami, home of hucksters, artists, beach bums, spring breakers, crypto-bros, alligators, posers, celebrities, roller bladers, plastic surgeons, sex workers, philosopher kings, oh, and poor little old me.

Don't worry, this isn't the kind of once-upon-a-time where I tell you all about how my great-grandmother Doña Edelira Maria Pérez Martinez castrated one of Fidel's proteges with a pair of rusty gardening shears before ferrying her clan, bloodied but largely intact, from the Cuba they had known for generations to seek refuge in the land of stars and stripes, establishing what was initially meant to be a temporary foothold in Miami as they watched with horror and bitterness and a surfeit of strong opinions while the *communistas* ran their beloved homeland into the ground. While the compounding surnames and melodrama of my family history could fill one thousand years of solitude, let alone García Márquez's measly hundred, and while it would surely provide a rich and textured backdrop against which to view my own donning of the cloak and unsheathing of the dagger in the name of Freedom (make sure to read the fine print), this isn't a story about a boy overcoming his humble origins (in case you haven't noticed, humility has never been one of my strengths, nor my family's) to rescue a princess from a dragon's lair. This is a story about two people locked in a room with a gun. Or, if you want to get metaphorical, this is a story about two dragons laying waste to whatever bucolic villages stand in the way of hunting each other down and using those scything dragon hind-claws to cut through those supposedly impenetrable dragon scales like warm butter and rip out each other's precious dragon entrails. Basically, a fairy tale right up the Grimm brothers' alley. Have you actually read that shit? It's *dark*.

So there I was sipping a sweet-as-sin cafecito in the bucolic village of Miami waiting for my contact to show. Lorenzo was a banker from Buenos Aires who supplemented his meager salary by finding creative ways to skim the cream off IMF loans that were intended to improve the general welfare of his countrymen and selling juicy rumors overheard in the *Casa Rosada* to whoever was willing to pay. At the end of the nineteenth century, Argentina was one of the wealthiest countries on Earth, living fat off cattle exports rolling in from the far-flung pampas on shiny new railroads. Now, it had become the kind of chronic clusterfuck that remains a clusterfuck because people excuse their clusterfuckery by pointing out how much of a clusterfuck it all is anyway. In other words, precisely the kind of country in which Uncle Sam and the rest of the not-so-very-United Nations like to meddle, to the detriment of all.

"Another cortado, sir?" asked the barista at the hole-in-the-wall coffee bar with the micro-roaster growling in the back like a chrome-enameled '50s muscle car.

I checked the time. Lorenzo was twenty-three minutes late. If he made me miss the connection back to DC, I was not going to be happy. Maybe I'd ask Leia to dock the fee she'd be squeezing through a series of shell companies and encryption layers to land in his Cayman Islands account. If someone didn't put their foot down, all the professionalism would leak out of the espionage scene. It's not enough to have the goods, you have to have the goods and be on time. Mutual respect. Am I right or am I right?

"Sure, why not?" I said. "Thanks..." I let the final syllable trail off into silence to give her room to fill it.

She obliged: "Caroline."

"Thanks, Caroline."

Lorenzo never showed.

The only thing sweeter than the second *cafecito* was the sex that followed.

Needless to say, I missed my flight.

5

Coital afterglow spiraled down the drain with the shower's steaming water, leaving behind a burgeoning resentment. Lorenzo loved to play things fast and loose. He enjoyed being Buenos Aires' favorite playboy, and needed the cash we paid for juicy whispers to support the opulent lifestyle he was known for and had become accustomed to. But when everyone treats you like a hot commodity, it's easy to forget that you are a *commodity*. You start believing what sycophants tell you. You lose your grip on the fundamentals. And the fundamentals in this particular case were that Lorenzo had made a lucrative business of selling intel to me, and people like me, but success was blinding him to the fact that the customer is always right. This wasn't the first time that he'd missed a meeting with me, but I was going to make damn sure it was the last.

I toweled off and emerged from the bathroom to discover that the barista had already left. There's another thing spy movies get wrong about espionage. Hollywood makes the casual sex seem exhilarating without pausing to consider how temporary that exhilaration is, and what it lacks. The truth is that a lifestyle of constant travel, secrets, and lies precludes pretty much any human connection deeper than a one-night stand, so you fill the void you're pretending doesn't exist with exotic but fleeting seductions.

Caroline's absence mixed me an emotional cocktail of disappointment, relief, and an abiding sense of vacancy. Now I didn't need to invent excuses, but not needing to invent excuses made me want to have had to invent excuses. As for Caroline, she hadn't even bothered to invent excuses of her own, which inspired a kind of grudging admiration. The more of a handle you think you have on desire, the more of a handle it has on you.

If only I had known. If only I could send my past self a text: "Forget Lorenzo, follow Caroline" or "That one-night stand is about to change your rotten life" or "Have fun? You're gonna end up interrogating each other at gunpoint" or even just "RED ALERT." But time is a stubborn motherfucker—it moves in one direction with a ruthless tenacity that even the most focused pro athlete can only dream of—so I let Caroline slip away and pursued my original quarry.

Suppressing instinctive distaste, I dressed in a floral-print

Hawaiian shirt, khaki shorts, white socks, sneakers, and aviator sunglasses—an outfit that would ensure others peg me as a tourist and instantly wipe me from their short-term memory. It was time to pack Lorenzo's carrots into the back of the crisper drawer and break out the hefty, gnarled stick.

Lorenzo was not at the backup location we'd previously established. He wasn't at his hotel. He wasn't at the South Beach bar where he loved to drink Negronis and tell dirty jokes. Nor was he at his favorite diner, the IMAX, the Argentinian consulate, or his second cousin's condo.

So much for taking him by surprise.

Yes, at this point I was trying to be flippant, but as you can probably tell, I was trying a little too hard. The truth was that my frustration had curdled into worry, and my concerns were escalating with every failed attempt to locate him.

Just like you don't want to lose track of your toddler at the supermarket, I didn't want to lose track of my source. Well, it's not *exactly* like that. Lorenzo wasn't a child of my loins, and we've already been over the fact that his intel outshone his personality, but it's generally frowned upon for spies to let their agents go missing. Worse, it meant I was missing something. Lorenzo's absence introduced an unknown variable into the complex series of equations my life depended on. And let me tell you, nothing scares people working in intelligence more than newfound ignorance.

So, over the next three days, I got serious.

6

Unfortunately, the more serious I got, the more serious the situation became.

Lorenzo had, in fact, landed on his scheduled flight and checked in at his usual hotel at the appointed time. So he was in Miami. But he had not engaged the exclusive services of any of the top seventeen escorts in the metropolitan area. He had not purchased drugs—not even really fun ones!—from any high-end local distributors. He hadn't used any of his credit or debit cards in the past seventy-two hours. He wasn't in any of the regional hospitals or morgues. He hadn't flown out from any of the surrounding airports under any known aliases, nor had their systems recognized his face in security footage. Ditto for outbound trains and buses. He hadn't rented a car, he hadn't entered the port, and he hadn't accessed any marinas that kept records.

I discreetly called in favors from childhood friends who'd made their way into law enforcement. I quietly used all the clandestine tools America had put at my disposal. I let bribes flow like the Nile. Nothing. And then more nothing. And some more nothing after that, with nothing dolloped on top. I found myself walking the streets hoping against hope that the next person to turn the corner, to exit the convenience store, to step out of the black SUV with tinted windows, to emerge laughing from the club with a pretty lady on each arm, would be Lorenzo.

Miami was all pastels and palm fronds and humidity. It was breakfast cocktails and braggadocio, sex and slander, fast money and slow afternoons. I grew up there. I knew how to swim in those waters. And I knew that under the sparkling rainbow palette lay desperation. Trailer park meth labs. Overloaded human trafficking networks. Abusive nursing homes. If actors are an essential part of what makes LA, and bankers are part of what makes New York New York, then plastic surgeons are part of what makes Miami Miami. We can make you beautiful. We can cover up the pain. We can cheat the reaper. But Botox robs you of expression even as it irons out the wrinkles—you end up with a face as exquisitely dead as marble.

One of my burners buzzed as I downed the last of my passionfruit juice. Boutique narcotics vendor. A couple of customers getting stratospherically high down at the docks had discovered a manatee playing with a bloated corpse matching the description I'd offered. They hadn't reported it to the authorities. Yet. Also, they were seventeen years old and hormonally unreliable, especially when said hormones got mixed up with hallucinogens and dead bodies. What did I want done?

I ditched the phone and made haste.

No matter what you tell yourself, the reaper takes his due.

7 ≡≡≡≡≡≡≡≡

≡≡≡≡≡≡≡ **Discreetly disposing of a dead body** is harder than you think.

If I had been deployed overseas, it would have been easy. Or, if not easy, at least straightforward. The agency has a network of reliable contractors the world over for sticky situations like this one. The bane of any forensics unit, they are fast, effective, and well worth their not insignificant fees. Get into a high-casualty shootout in drug trafficker's beach house? They'll sweep the entire thing and leave it spick and span and ready to post on Airbnb in under seventy-two minutes.

Sadly, these consummate professionals were not an option. I was on US soil, and there are a bunch of very annoying rules about spies like me running ops like this on home turf. Technically, we're supposed to do things like notify the FBI, which, like, no. Never. Seriously? Gross. Of course, these rules don't actually prevent spies like me from running ops like this on home turf. The rules just mean that instead of spying with the institutional backing of our nation state, we have to improvise and spy like petty criminals.

So I purchased Costco quantities of drugs I didn't even realize existed from the dealer who'd tipped me off and used the goodies to recruit the three seventeen year olds into my temporary service. The kids were neither fast nor effective, but I needed help, and I didn't want to expand the circle of people who knew something had gone down. Plus, their unreliability would hinder any subsequent investigation even more than it hindered me. It took three and a half hours, and more than three and a half pep talks, but we managed to wrap the body in heavy-duty garbage bags, load it into a stolen RV, and torch it with the help of an insolvent crematorium desperate for cash.

I gave the kids a bonus, suggested they write off the whole episode as a bad trip (which it certainly had been), and watched them scurry away into the sunset. Then I turned on my heels and let my feet take me wherever they wanted to go.

It really was a spectacular sunset. Clouds piled up into fluffy towers and smeared across the sky, the dying light making them appear to glow from within across an opulent spectrum of amber, crimson, and magenta. Birds sang and soared and swooped. The air was thick, the breeze warm, the world brimming over with itself.

In that overwhelming everything, I was a pocket of nothing, a gap in the firmament. This was the first time I'd been able to take a moment to breathe in the three days since Lorenzo disappeared. When something goes that wrong, there is no room for feeling, only action. You don't think. You *do*. And then you keep doing and doing until fate decides to back off a bit. Only then can you afford to ease off, to process whatever you can before the next thing goes wrong.

8

My feet took me into the adjoining cemetery, a tropical oasis where palms and jacarandas threw long shadows across stubby headstones and hulking mausoleums. Lorenzo wouldn't get ferried across the river Styx with such ceremony. He would suffer the indignity of disappearance, his friends and family left with an open question instead of closure. He didn't deserve it. It wasn't fair. But he'd chosen to play games where there was no such thing as fair play, and when you played that kind of game and lost, the people who loved you paid the price. Hell, when you played that kind of game and *won*, the people who loved you *still* paid the price.

Dusk deepened into darkness. Sunken lights came on along the sides of the path, creating little golden pools of illumination. The surrounding city receded, a separate world. The world of the living.

I had cleaned up a mess that could have escalated into an international incident, but that didn't mean my boss was going to like it. Leia abhorred anything that might threaten her rise through the intersecting circles of Beltway power. This Lorenzo situation was precisely that kind of problem, which meant she might already be setting me up as the fall guy.

The whole point was to avoid a scandal, so she'd do it quietly. Reassign me to administrative bullshit, or cut me loose with severance to seek my fortune as a contractor. I imagined tapping sources for consulting fees, making competitive intelligence slide decks, bolstering my cred by telling veiled war stories to mid-level executives over stale Starbucks coffee. Fucking bleak. I'd be better off teaming up with those teenagers to turn my neurochemistry into a Fourth of July fireworks display.

When you go all-in on your job because your job is to protect what makes your country great, then losing your job means losing everything. You go from unsung hero to unsung dirtbag. All those relationships you never cultivated, all those opportunities you didn't take, all those hard truths you never told, all those lives you never lived amount to nothing at all. Jack shit. Zilch. Thanks for your sacrifice, now fuck off. Enjoy binging YouTube until the algorithm eats your soul.

I came to a halt and let out a breath I didn't realize I'd been holding. My feet had delivered me to my abuela's grave. She'd indulged herself in one of her signature tight-lipped smiles when she managed to call in enough favors and pull enough strings to secure a family plot here in the sought-after Miami City Cemetery. For her, it was a statement, as if the only way to put down roots was to fertilize them with bones.

I knelt in the grass and ran my fingers across the headstone's engravings. Names. Dates. Poetry. Cuba had betrayed her, and, in Miami, she had found not only refuge, but a fierce pride in what her adoptive home stood for. That's what I had devoted myself to defending. If I was stripped of my role in its defense, then who would I even be?

My phone buzzed. An abrupt, alien intrusion.

It was Leia. Of course it was.

"Come home," she texted. "Now."

I swore with unbridled creativity, kissed the headstone, and returned to the world of the living.

9

Leia is from California. Try not to hold it against her.

One of the Marin County habits she can't seem to kick is walking meetings. At first, it drove me nuts. How many strolls along the Potomac do you really need in one lifetime? Tell me what I need to know and let's move on already. Leave the forest to the squirrels. But then the beige carpeting and terrible lighting and infinite PowerPoints and bad coffee and feigned attention and shameless preemptive ass-covering in an endless sequence of Langley conference rooms blended together into a bland abyss far beyond the scope of Dante's Inferno and I suddenly saw merit in Leia's New-Agey walk-and-talks.

It was a spectacular morning, as if the universe was cheerfully trying to spite me as I faced the premature implosion of my professional life. It would have been unfortunate but understandable if I'd played a big hand and lost. Maybe by acting on a hunch that would have secured nuclear codes if things hadn't gone terribly wrong, or even by being outmaneuvered by a clever rival. But this? This was just such a dumb way to go. It felt simultaneously melodramatic and anticlimactic.

Birds were literally chirping, and while it was unnerving to discuss Lorenzo's grisly fate in the midst of what appeared to be a Hallmark card championing the natural beauty of Northern Virginia, the surreal juxtaposition of pathos and pizzaz reminded me of my abuela's favorite salsa tunes, so my subconscious tapped out the clave to accompany the report I really, really didn't want to deliver.

As bosses go, Leia is generally a good one. By that I mean she is maniacally obsessed with clawing to the top of the DC pile, no matter who she has to crush to get there. I find the entire Beltway scene to be a soul-sucking bore inhabited by self-aggrandizing desk jockeys jerking each other off for the chance to spend five minutes playing with a powerbroker's puppet strings. I live for the field. Jetting off to exotic lands. Trading secrets like Pokémon. Thumbing the scales of history. Leia sees the field as a dirty and mildly distasteful place to waste a career. Happily, we recognize these qualities in each other. I know not to get in the way of her blazing ascent through the hopelessly tangled intelligence community org chart, and she knows to give me enough leash to hang myself when it comes to practical matters like bribing border guards, ferrying fugitives through enemy territory, or developing sources at schmancy diplomatic cocktail parties.

This was the symbiotic dynamic that made me and Leia such effective copilots of the espionage airliner, but Lorenzo was an unlucky seagull sucked into our jet engine. My agent had been unceremoniously offed by an unknown party. Worse, it transpired on American soil. Worse still, I had failed to notify the appropriate counterintelligence "partners" of the operation, putting Leia in the awkward position of either apologizing to the FBI (cringe) or risking her reputation to cover it up.

As I walked her through what had happened beat by beat, I started drafting my letter of resignation in my head. Most people write generic resignation letters, but this would be my last act as an intelligence officer. I would make mine good. In all likelihood, no one would ever read it. But if they did, I wanted them to know what doing what I did meant to me, what it was to be a spy, and where leaving the game would leave me.

A trio of monarchs flitted by through the dappled light.

No, I'm not even messing with you: Fucking. Butterflies.

The only thing missing was a David Attenborough voiceover.

Ever the gentleman, I neglected to mention the carnal delights of my one-night stand. It just didn't feel necessary to mention getting laid during a career-ending debrief. Let the record show that it's the lies of omission that always come back to bite you in the ass.

10

I concluded my report by asking Leia to let me return to Miami to search for the clues that FBI investigators would be guaranteed to overlook, i.e. anything that lay even marginally outside the painstakingly enumerated box they all seem to inhabit, sentenced to life, as they are, in the maximum security prison of small-mindedness.

It's not that I wanted to avenge Lorenzo or WD-40 the chronically squeaky scales of justice. The problem was that I didn't anticipate his murder. Lorenzo was killed for a reason. I wanted to know what that reason was and, I pointed out, so should Leia.

If you have friends who work in intelligence, do *not* throw them surprise birthday parties. One of two things will happen. Either they'll discover your plans and ruin the effect, or you'll take them by surprise and leave their nerves jangling for the next eighteen months. As they blow out the candles they'll be wondering who else might be ensnaring them in a secret plot given that *you* were able to pull off such a feat with a roomful of amateurs. The moral of the story is that getting blindsided sucks if you're professionally paranoid, and I was quite keen to find a vantage from which to gaze upon this particular blindside so as to nullify it.

I wanted to draw the story out, delay the fall of the ax by talking and talking and talking some more. But I'd been raised to look the devil in the eye, so I said my piece, shut my mouth, and steeled my heart.

Leia looked me straight in the eye and said, "Can I trust you?"

Which is, like, offensive. I knew she'd be mad. I hadn't guessed she'd be mad enough to stoop to this level of insult.

"WTF, Leia?" I demanded before I could stop myself. "Of course you can't trust me. We're spooks, not dilettantes. Now you have me seriously worried that you're losing your touch."

She held my gaze, then gave a single, curt nod.

"Alright," she said. "How good of a spook are you?"

"The fucking best," I said with the absolute conviction of the condemned.

"Alright," she said again. "Then I can't afford to waste you on playing detective for Lorenzo."

"But–"

She held up a hand to forestall my objections.

"There's a mission that needs the fucking best," she said. "Pack your bags. You're going to Mindanao."

"Look," I said, heart falling. Here it was: the ticket to nowhere. "I lost a source. You're pissed. I get it. But Abu Sayyaf? You don't need to bench me. Or even if you do need to bench me, can you bench me somewhere that doesn't require chasing pissant insurgents through a mosquito-infested jungle? I've already had dengue once, and it's supposed to be worse the second time around."

Leia gave me a pitying look. "You won't be hunting Abu Sayyaf," she said. "They're far too convenient a cover for our little operation. The last thing we want to do is eliminate them."

"Then what will I be doing?"

Leia might be from California, but her hard smile had been baked in DC's kiln.

"More than you signed up for," she said.

MC Escher was throwing me a surprise birthday party inside a surprise birthday party inside a surprise birthday party on and on forever and I did *not* appreciate it.

11

Already running late for her next meeting, Leia took the next trail that forked back to headquarters. I watched her disappear and then chose a path at random and followed it through the woods.

Shafts of sunlight penetrated the leafy canopy to dapple the mossy rocks and gnarled roots underfoot. The air was thick with the rich smell of loam. Squirrels chattered somewhere above. Dew glittered on fern fronds.

It felt like walking a maze. You couldn't see more than a dozen feet in any direction through the lush foliage. The path might take you on and on for miles. It might split and split and split again. It might lead you straight into a dead end. Or it might loop back on itself forever, leaving you to spend the rest of your days hiking into the cloying fog of déjà vu.

None of this made any sense. Leia was notorious for unleashing reprimands that could take down an ego as efficiently as a demolition man does a derelict skyscraper. She was the kind of shepherd who wouldn't hesitate to cleave any stragglers from her flock. But when I'd disclosed my fuckup, the rare kind of fuckup that could threaten her position, she'd ignored it completely. I had been preparing to survive a nuclear winter but been handed an ice cream cone instead.

That isn't how these things are supposed to go.

The forest brightened around me and then I came around a bend and emerged onto the bank of the Potomac. The placid river stretched out before me like a mirror, reflecting the sky and giving the disorienting impression of standing on a celestial shore, clouds hanging below my feet.

I knelt, selected a wide, flat stone, wound up, and skipped it. One. Two. Three-four-five. Six. Seven. The ripples fanned out, intersecting each other, erasing the reflected sky. Again. One-two-three. Four. Five. Again. One-two. Three-four. Five. Six. Seven. Eight-Nine.

Pristine heavens above.

Disturbed waters below.

Me in the middle, wondering what exactly I had gotten myself into. I wanted the ice cream cone. I really did. But ice cream can be laced with nastier concoctions than fudge.

12

There are secrets, and then there are Secrets.

When you glance at your classmate's answers on a geometry exam, that's a secret. When you tell a buddy you
already have (nonexistent) dinner plans because you can't
abide his girlfriend, that's a secret. We all have secrets.
Maybe you skipped ahead and watched an episode of the
Netflix series you and your husband are supposed to be
binging together. Maybe your favorite ice cream flavor
is vanilla, which you don't admit to anyone for fear of
coming across as unimaginative. I harbor an unreason-
able hatred for pastel polo shirts, for example. If I am
unlucky enough to find myself in a New England yacht
club in summer, I have to suppress the urge to punch every

polo-ed prick right in prominent Adam's apple bobbing up and down between the flared ends of the inevitably popped collar. I once humiliated a boy who tried to kiss me, for which I still feel ashamed—I do hope he's found a better man than me. Oh, and I roll my eyes during briefings when Leia isn't looking. A secret might disrupt your life, but it won't change your future.

A Secret, on the other hand, exerts a gravitational pull on your destiny. When you cheat on your husband, that's a Secret. When you fabricate your résumé for a job application, that's a Secret. When you don't just buy drugs, but sell them. When you discover the CFO's master password scribbled on a scrap of paper under her desk. When you dox the upstart trying to steal your congressional seat. Only some people have Secrets.

Mostly assholes like me.

But Secrets aren't just things I've buried deep enough in my psyche to slowly corrode my conscience. They're my stock in trade. They come in an infinite variety of flavors: weapons designs, details of ongoing business negotiations, royal gossip, SVR dead drop locations, jealously guarded algorithms, transcripts of clandestine treaties, who's fucking whom at the nuclear power plant, satellite coordinates, the Coca Cola recipe, what would make the perfect gift for a particular head of state, Satoshi Nakamoto's true identity, which Saudi prince likes to attend BDSM parties in Berlin, etc., etc. Welcome to my gelateria. Would you like to taste them all? They will make you swoon.

And now you know why being a spy is so intoxicating: it offers a profound and enduring feeling of superiority.

You know things others don't. Your business is making everyone else's business your business. You are the master of revelation. The only downside is that you are also its slave. That, and the more aces you stuff up your sleeve, the more you want to play them, and the more casino security wants to catch you.

Mindanao wasn't a secret.

It wasn't even a Secret.

It was a SECRET.

13

I arrived via submarine, and if you think that's over-the-top, just wait till you hear what came next.

It was a small submarine: a personal submersible. An F-16 flew me out to an aircraft carrier running an exercise in the South China Sea. A helicopter ferried me to one of the destroyers hovering in formation around the carrier like flies around a water buffalo. From there, I was hustled onto a small patrol boat which quickly motored away from the flotilla. We rendezvoused with what looked like a dilapidated local trawler complete with intractable crew, diesel fumes, and fish guts. After a few hours of chugging through rolling groundswell (thankfully, I'm not prone to seasickness), we approached a rugged coastline hemmed in by lush rainforest, massive thunderheads rearing up behind a distant volcano. Only then did the piratical captain lead me below decks where my personal submersible waited in its camouflaged launch bay.

I still can't decide whether it was a torpedo shaped like a coffin or a coffin shaped like a torpedo. Either way, I was grateful that it could pilot itself and knew where it was going, because by that point I was loopy with jet lag and shuttling between vehicles. My coffin/torpedo launched with a whoosh and then hummed through the depths as I prayed to Poseidon for safe passage and tried not to imagine the shark-infested ocean breaking through the seals protecting my little life-support bubble. I'm not normally claustrophobic, but this was an extremely confined space. Plus, torpedoes imply hull breaches, and coffins imply corpses.

So it was with great relief that I sucked in a deep breath when my submersible chimed, the hatch hissed open, and I sat up like a vampire rising from a thousand-year slumber. The air smelled faintly of minerals and lavender. Verdant jungle rose up on all sides. The undergrowth was impenetrable. Hummingbirds dive-bombed through hanging vines. A spectacular orchid caught a stray beam of sunlight. Through the canopy's interstices I could see the thunderheads I'd observed from the trawler advancing across the baby blue sky. The submersible must have navigated some kind of submarine cave system to reach this briny pool in the middle of a small clearing. I was starting to wonder why someone had built what was clearly a well-maintained dock on the edge of a pool in the middle of a remote corner of the rainforest when I spotted Leia.

She looked down at me quizzically from a gap in the foliage, head tilted slightly to one side, hands clasped behind her back.

"Pleasant trip?" she asked with a raised eyebrow.

14

Leia had briefed me immediately before liftoff in DC. How had she beaten me here? "The in-flight snacks on the fighter jet were subpar," I said. "But nothing rocks me to sleep like a one-man submarine fighting a side-shore current." Still sitting in the open submersible, I arched my back like a cat, working hard to hide how surprised I was to see her.

"I'm glad to see your snark arrived intact," she said.

"Snark? I'm earnest through and through," I said. If she wanted to keep on pretending what happened in Miami hadn't happened, I was happy to hold up my end of the charade. "Always on the up-and-up. Nothing but sincere." I knew one thing for sure: they wouldn't have gone to the effort of getting me here this way if this was just some hole to bury me in. You don't ferry someone to a cul-de-sac on an F-16. "Though I must admit to being sincerely miffed that you didn't invite me to accompany you on whatever forking paths led you to this little pocket of primeval forest. Nothing enriches a journey like a fellow traveler. Is my charm too refined to risk prolonged exposure?"

The mischievous delight in Leia's grin had sent a chill down the spine of many a sitting senator. My charm, being what it was, rarely elicited such a reaction from this particular alpha predator, which meant that either I was being even more winsome than usual (probable), or she had another reason for her high good humor (sadly, even more probable, and, needless to say, worrying).

Leia waved her hand.

The teeming jungle vanished.

Evanescent northern lights writhed against the black abyss of space, flaring green and purple and blue as they knit the sky into a single vast display that put the most ambitious of EDM festivals to shame. The aurorae reflected off the vast snow field that spread out around us in all directions, the glittering expanse interrupted by scattered glades of dark evergreens, needles sheathed in ice.

The submersible rocked beneath me as I locked the edges of the hatch in a death grip, reeling.

Leia waved her hand again.

Merciless desert sun blazed down on us. Joshua Trees rose from the desolate landscape like spiny denizens of a Dr. Seuss story, straining their shaggy arms toward the dome of polished cerulean sky. Piles of jagged boulders littered open swaths of coarse sand like the abandoned building blocks of a bored titan.

Again.

We perched on the peak of a high mountain, the ridge running before and behind us to yet more peaks. To one side, clouds boiled below, kinetic tufts kissed pink by breaking dawn. To the other, shale fell away steeply toward manzanita, distant meadows dotted with a dozen small lakes, everything cast in shades of alpine shadow.

My breath came fast and shallow. I could still smell the lavender, which, while it reminded me of my abuela's lemonade, was not a scent I associate with rainforest, tundra, desert, or mountaintops. Also, neither the temperature nor the humidity had changed during our rapid-fire teleportation.

"This is some Harry Potter shit," I said. "Or maybe you're using the Force. Have you finally reclaimed your Skywalker heritage?"

Yes, I realize that humor is a coping mechanism.

"Welcome to Mindanao," she said. "Shall I give you the tour?"

"Whatever this is, you're enjoying it a little too much, boss," I said, trying to bring my heart rate under control.

"It's the small pleasures that make life worth living," she said.

I steadied the submersible. First things first. Disembark. I could worry about my existential crisis after I was back on solid ground. "Give a guy a hand?"

"Wish I could," she said. "But I'm seven thousand miles away."

15

Imagine a bunch of grapes hanging underground. That was the basic layout of the Mindanao facility: a preexisting cave system had been converted into a network of roughly globular rooms connected by angled passageways. Each resident had a small cell that functioned as bedroom and private workspace. There was a shared kitchen with a lounge, communal bathrooms, a gym, and—because apparently even the most clandestine of secret bases is built around and for the bane of my existence: meetings—a conference room. The bottommost grape in the bunch was the sea-cave dock where I'd arrived, and there were multiple hidden access points into the jungle above.

The curved walls and ceilings of every room were lined with some kind of seamless display I'd never seen before, the slick inner surface of each grape skin a membrane to the digital infinite. The landscapes through which Leia had transported me, and Leia herself, had been visions woven from silicon, fiber, and light, my boss projecting herself to a remote corner of the Philippines from her office in Langley. Now that I could parse what I was looking at, and wasn't emerging bleary-eyed from an autonomous water coffin, I could just barely distinguish between pixels and reality via subtle anomalies of depth and perspective, but the verisimilitude was astounding—many orders of magnitude better than what Hollywood was able to conjure.

Precise climate control kept the humidity pleasant and the temperature on the cool end of comfortable, hidden vents wafting faux breezes, the signature scents of lavender and minerals implying that we might be relaxing in an open-air grotto in the South of France. Every room was soundproof, and even with the doors open, the corridors were engineered to dampen sound, an understated effect that reinforced the impression that this was a network of spaces.

Leia gave me the tour, her avatar waiting for me in each room's pocket universe as I traversed the adjoining passage. In an apparent effort to make me feel at home, my cell was set to the North Point of Virginia Key, Miami glittering behind its seawalls across the South Channel like a nouveau riche engagement ring. I didn't want to think about Lorenzo, and the skyline was precisely familiar enough to render the experience yet more uncanny, so I had Leia switch it to Joshua Tree, which was basically an alien planet to begin with, and therefore, by being more weird, made me feel less weird about what was an objectively weird situation.

All in all, the production values were way too high for government work, or, put another way, if this was government work, there must be an extraordinarily compelling reason for the production values to be this high. I'm no general contractor, but extravagant subterranean holodecks can't come cheap. So as Leia led me around what was to be my home for the next few months and introduced me to my new roommates, I tried to dispel the mental fog of shock and jet lag.

What was this place for?

And why was I here?

16

The other residents were called "Residents," which was both profoundly unimaginative and weirdly echoed the Russian nomenclature for a station chief: *rezident*. But hey, they don't ask me when they name programs or coin acronyms—and I hope they never ask me, because then I'd have to brainstorm a bunch of dumb options myself, and probably make some slides with tacky fonts, and practice "stakeholder engagement" in order to "build alignment" and "iterate based on feedback" until I wound up with the same boring, off-key language I'm complaining about. Ugh. Leave bureaucracy to the bureaucrats.

Speaking of bureaucracy—have I piqued your curiosity? It's hard to imagine a more titillating segue—each

Resident represented a branch of the good ol' US Government: Samantha for DoD, Bisrat for NSA, Jerry for State (which, like, *really?*), and, finally—saving the best for last—me for CIA.

Despite the embarrassing inclusion of a career diplomat, the company was, in fact, quite exclusive. No records were kept of the facility or its personnel. Everything was funded under a black budget. We did not exist. We failed to exist to a sufficient extent that we entered and exited this subterranean zone of liminal oblivion via submersibles. My fellow nonexistent Residents were serious people, and I could tell by the way that Leia introduced me that this was important to her, important enough that she was doing everything she could not to show it, least of all to me, but then, if I was the kind of person who wouldn't notice that kind of thing, I wouldn't be the kind of person she'd send here in the first place. If you've ever struggled managing a team, be they dodgeball players or management consultants, imagine how bad it would be if you were stuck managing spies. We're just the absolute worst.

If this was important to Leia, it could mean only one thing: her career was on the line. Whatever this was, she'd risked a lot to secure a slot for her pawn (i.e. me). And that meant that she *saw* me as her pawn, a variable substantially within her control, which made *me* see her inexplicable pivot during our forest walk along the Potomac in a new light.

She hadn't been taking heat from her bosses about Lorenzo. She hadn't even *told* her bosses about Lorenzo. She hadn't wanted me to go to Miami to follow up because then I couldn't have helped but notice the obvious lack of an investigation into his death. No. Leia had taken advantage of my quick disposal of the body and smoothed everything over. Knowing her, she would have had many reasons to do so. She's not the kind of person who does things for merely one reason. But at least one of her reasons would have been to add it to the list of things she could hold over me to ensure that if and when things went sideways, I'd do what she wanted.

I told you: she's good.

And if you're all, like, "My good sir, that smells like a steaming pile of brontosaurus manure to me. How dare you accuse your colleague—your *superior officer*—based on, at best, circumstantial evidence," then please believe me when I tell you that espionage isn't a game where you're innocent until proven guilty. It's a game where the guilty play innocent, and the innocent get framed.

Just ask any *rezident*.

17

Do you know the story of Damocles?

There's this city, Syracuse, on the east coast of Sicily. Greek settlers established a colony there in the eighth century BCE. So the king of Syracuse, Dionysius, loves hosting these opulent feasts, and he has this courtier, Damocles, who's a total party-boy yes-man, classic entourage material.

One day, they're chugging wine and fondling servants and shooting the shit and Damocles says how fucking cool he thinks it must be to be king. The crown! The throne! The *power*! Must be nice, huh?

Now, you might expect a tyrant like Dionysius to take this opportunity to shut his boy down: bro, don't even *think* about it. But no, Dionysius says: oh, *this*? Sovereignty? You want to try it? Be my guest, hombre.

So Dionysius sets Damocles up on the throne. He places the crown on his head. He makes sure Damocles is offered the most succulent wild boar, the finest wine, the most lyrical poetry, the softest silks, the deepest obeisance, and, crucially, the hottest servants.

Damocles is thinking, *fuck yeah, this is what I was talking about*, but then he glances up and sees that right above his head is a razor-sharp sword hanging by a single strand of horsehair, and he immediately and shamelessly begs Dionysius to take back the kingship ASAP.

Politicians love to hijack a good metaphor. JFK warned the UN about the threat of nuclear war by saying, "Every man, woman and child lives under a nuclear sword of Damocles hanging by the slenderest of threads." Referencing the classics is a tried and true technique for bulking up your gravitas, except that in this case the story isn't about impending apocalypse—it's far more interesting than that.

The moral of Damocles's story is to beware envying the lives of the powerful, for a life of power is a life lived in terror.

Leia is a Dionysius. She sharpens swords, hangs them from horse hairs, and lures the Damocleses of the world onto thrones, thrones she stands behind with a pair of scissors, shaping the course of history with whispers. I am one of her Damocleses. Lorenzo is just the latest example—Leia has dirt on me going back a good long way. I've always been her right hand in the field while she's always shielded me from internal politics, which has been enormously convenient for both of us, but which also means that if she ever decides to fuck me, I will be well and truly fucked because I have no institutional cachet with which to thwart an internal attack on my reputation. But that's OK, because I know it, and I know it because I am a Dionysius to many Damocleses of my own: sources and agents scattered across all seven continents (yes, even a melancholic glaciologist stationed at Esperanza Base, Antartica).

Like recognizes like, and our vocation is a hall of mirrors with dagger chandeliers.

But we are not the only ones who should heed the story's warning. In reading this account, you may find yourself wondering what it might be like to be a spy. Secrets. Intrigue. Adventure. A sense that the risks are worth it because they feel important, they matter, they are the stakes that are missing from your conference calls, your overflowing inbox, your next deadline. What would you do if you found yourself in my shoes? Maybe you would feel that ineffable *something* that your own life can't seem to muster.

Daydream all you want, dear reader, but never forget: you can't extract the terror from the power.

18

"**Don't fuck this up,**" Leia said, and vanished, leaving me staring off into a barren desert fashioned from pixels instead of sand.

The desert was good, though. Perhaps my overflowing mind could spill into it, flooding its dunes and filling its sky. I'd been expecting to be kicked to the curb, but instead I'd been catapulted into a fortress of covert power. It was like getting assigned to the first Mars mission after spending every minute of your precious life training to become an astronaut. I had so many questions. I had so many ideas. I had so many doubts and fears and aspirations. I didn't deserve to be here. I didn't want to be anywhere but here. It was a lot. Too much. At least the desert distracted me from the fact that I was sitting on the edge of my bed in a tiny inhabitable bubble surrounded by megatons of volcanic rock, although recognizing the distraction for what it was undermined its efficacy.

Don't fuck this up.

"This" was the key word: Operation Glass Ceiling.

The United States of America was a young nation. Bootstrapped on conquest, slavery, and revolution (political, intellectual, technological, commercial, social, etc.), it displaced the older powers that had birthed it when Europe tore itself apart in back-to-back world wars and the US roared in to fill the economic vacuum. The Soviet Union was an irresistible sparring partner for a few decades before collapsing under its own weight, leaving America to rest easy in hegemony.

But hegemony slips away from those who rest easy. As soon as you take something for granted, fate revokes the grant. The US drained its coffers on useless wars and bitter infighting, failing to tackle problems of sufficient ambition to lead the world, instead of merely ruling it—not unlike the progeny of a wealthy family blowing their inheritance on yacht parties, space tourism, and fraternal rivalry.

China stepped in to fill the gap, remixing conventional "isms" of political economy into a potent national cocktail that lifted millions out of poverty, established a tightly controlled domestic internet, anchored global supply chains, centralized power into fewer and fewer hands, oppressed ethnic minorities, and secured a leading role on the world stage.

Nothing stokes the insecurities of a reigning champion like the sudden appearance of a rising star, and Washington and Beijing transitioned smoothly from economic cooperation to discreet sabotage, waging a new kind of cold war with packets of code, foreign aid, trade disputes, zero days, and press conferences.

In this war, Operation Glass Ceiling was the front line, and its mission was to construct its namesake—invisibly thwarting the aspirations of America's ascendant rival. We were an autonomous cell outside the formal chain of command—giving us radical agility and our masters blessed deniability—yet each Resident could summon the powers vested in the particular faction they represented.

If we were discovered, we wouldn't just be disowned, we'd be erased. But as long as we stayed hidden, we were as gods. The digital envelopes we inhabited could display more than landscapes: we could conjure any scrap of intelligence the US Government had ever collected. We could run operations anywhere on Earth. We could put a price on anyone's head. As long as it was in service of reining in Beijing, we could do whatever we could get away with, which was less a constraint than a challenge.

No wonder Leia could barely contain her glee: this was where the action was, and I was her man on the ground.

Don't fuck this up.

Oh, if she only knew.

19

My therapist tells me I distance myself from what I care about to protect myself from getting hurt.

You may have noticed that I describe these extraordinary events from a certain remove, as if I were a fly on the wall instead of a fly in the ointment. I deflect. I lacquer truth with sarcasm. I wander off on tangents to buy time. I separate the world from what it means to me.

Do not take this to mean that I don't care.

I care.

I care a great deal.

I care so much that I am doing everything I possibly can to convince you that I don't care, because I know from experience that not caring about something is often the best way to get it. Of course, *pretending* not to care about something is much less effective. But reality is socially determined, so if I'm able to persuade you that I don't care, maybe I'll be able to trick myself into not caring for long enough to get what I want. It's a delicate line, though. If you trick yourself too well, you'll end up genuinely not caring about the thing you just worked so hard to get— imagine Galahad attaining the Holy Grail only to piss in it—so implement this strategy at your own risk.

What is it exactly that I care about so desperately that I'm compelled to hide it not just from you, but from myself? What is the want smoldering in the ash pit of my soul? What are the desires that define me, the goals I falsely imagine would complete me, the rabbit my heart's hound is trying to flush?

Dim the lights.

Cue the drumroll.

Lean in.

Ready.

Set.

G–

Seriously?! You're telling me you actually thought that I was going to tell you, of all people, what drives me? I literally just explained why I would never, ever do that. Even admitting it to myself would undermine everything I'm trying to achieve here.

Let's just say that I am very much in the ointment.

Aren't we all?

Oh, and no, of course I don't actually have a therapist.

I'm an intelligence agent. I know way too much to let someone inside my head, and my mind's warped labyrinth is a professional asset. But if I did have a therapist, they'd tell you that lying about having a therapist to create space for vulnerability is exactly the kind of dissociative behavior I claimed as my diagnosis.

20

Late one night, after all the other Residents had retired, I double checked that my door was locked, leaned back in my chair, and piloted my pod on a voyage across the digital seas in search of Lorenzo.

There was a lot. Birth certificate. Health records. School reports. Text chains. Email correspondence. Tax forms. Social media feeds. Tagged photos. Surveillance footage. Banking information. Search queries. Forum posts. Credit card details. Travel data. Brokerage accounts. Titles, deeds, trusts, and wills. Purchase history. Background checks. Tagged photos. Article mentions. On and on and on. The bountiful digital wake displaced by an indiscreet life.

It would take years for me to manually sort through this much information, but I wasn't trying to write Lorenzo's biography, I was searching for any clues that might indicate why he'd been killed. So I fed the data into Mozaik and started playing with prompts, iteratively nudging the AI to tease out signal from a storm of noise.

The results were... bullshit. And then more bullshit. And yet more bullshit. Nothing revelatory. Nothing I could use. Just inane correlations and recapitulations of obvious findings. I kept going, imagining the machine to be an inept dancing partner, showing it the steps, cultivating beginner's mind, encouraging it to feel the rhythm, giving it enough leash to make useful mistakes, smiling when it stomped on my toes, refining the approach instead of jumping to conclusions, letting it explore the possibility space until something raw and beautiful emerged.

Finally, just when I was ready to give up, something emerged.

Have you heard of Analog, the infamous off-grid social club in San Francisco? It's one of those members-only watering holes where politicians, hackers, CEOs, artists, scientists, brokers, fixers, poets, celebrities, gossip mongers, geniuses, and dilettantes mix and mingle, peddling influence, hatching plans, forging alliances, betraying confidences, and guzzling self-sabotaging quantities of top-shelf liquor. Analog takes its name seriously: there are no electronic devices allowed inside—in fact, they don't even use electricity; it's oil lamps for light, a hearth for heat, etc. Basically, pre-industrial LARPing. But the upshot is that the club is a tiny whirlpool of invisibility in the ocean of data my pod can safely navigate.

Lorenzo visited Analog. I can't tell you what happened inside, but I can tell you that, per usual, a diverse cast of the rich and powerful all happened to be there at the time. And I can tell you something else. The second Lorenzo exited the club and regained access to his phone, he messaged me to set up the meeting in Miami.

He had discovered something.

Something valuable enough to sell at auction.

Something valuable enough to kill for.

21

Jack up the volume and play your favorite pump-up track, because it's time for a montage.

Samantha, the ex-SEAL, trained me in armed and unarmed combat. Yes, I'd had combat training at The Farm, but I hadn't touched a weapon since, because when your business is intelligence, guns coming out means you've already failed. Despite what 007 might make you think, spying is about relationships, not shootouts. Nevertheless, by repeatedly kicking my ass with ruthless efficiency and meeting my failure-induced tantrums with beguiling calm, she leveled me up from pitiful to merely incompetent. It was deeply unpleasant, but violence always is. I politely requested that if she was ever ordered to kill me, she did so with a drone strike so I wouldn't see it coming.

Bisrat, the wizard from NSA, updated my digital trade-craft, cluing me in on how to evade or confuse the Eye of Sauron that was always glaring down the internet in my general direction. She briefed me on the evolving architecture of the Great Firewall, the state-backed and independent hacker groups that vied in this particular arena, and the surveillance capabilities where I might be deployed. Computer evangelists love to wax lyrical about how their gadgets will change the world, but sometimes it feels like the most significant change so far is that we've locked ourselves in a tower where we chase each other up and down staircases that interlock to infinity, leading nowhere. That said, the only thing worse than exploring those staircases with Bisrat would have been exploring them alone—without her expert guidance I would be well and truly fucked. So I shut my Luddite mouth and made copious notes.

Even Jerry—of course his name was Jerry—from State turned out to be useful. He buffed up my Mandarin and Cantonese, offered historical context for the current contest, explained the competing meta-narratives that propagandists on all sides were striving to shape, and honed my apparently barbaric table manners. To my everlasting frustration, Jerry was a genuinely good guy. I want to hate him so bad, but I just can't! When you're in the same room with him you can feel how the thing he wants most in the world is for you to become your best self. It's astounding that anyone like that wound up in a place like this, but somehow Jerry did. Good for you, Jerry. Actually, probably not, but there's not a whole lot I can do about it.

Leia beamed in from Langley to complement Jerry's briefings with intel from behind the scenes. Nestled in its ring roads, Beijing might appear monolithic to naive outsiders, but was just as riven by factions as the Beltway. Political machination is universal, and finding points of leverage is all about understanding the incentive systems you're interfacing with.

Everyone had something to offer, and I was a sponge soaking it all up. Whenever I wasn't being trained, I was either sleeping or teaching the group to dance salsa in the common room. Samantha was a natural, although I was worried she might reach around and snap my neck in time with the *clave*.

Oh, and another thing: the kitchen was equipped with a Nespresso machine. Do you have any idea how awful it is to live in a cave without access to real coffee? I'm not asking for a high-end Slayer. They could have stocked a pour-over setup or a French press or even an AeroPress. But no, our coffee was all pods, no beans. Yuck. I would have killed for a *cafetera*, and thanks to Samantha, I *could* have killed for one.

While you judge me for being the coffee snob that I unabashedly am, make sure your montage tune is reaching for its synth-laden climax, because after three months on this particular hamster wheel, it was time for me to get to work.

22

There's a special quality to summer fog rolling in off the Pacific, streaming through clefts, pooling in hollows, the leading edge feathering away in the chill, steady breeze: a sense of living inside a vast enigma that we rarely glimpse, and even then, indirectly.

I watched the fog through the glass wall of the posh Threshold cafeteria where I was waiting for Phillip, who was supposed to join me in exactly seven minutes and twenty-two seconds, having stolen a secret that could make him rich, or end his career. The pseudonymous guest badge hung heavy around my neck. Jargony conversation ebbed and flowed across the surrounding tables. The fresh *puntarelle* was more delicious than it had any right to be.

Silicon Valley.

Silicon Valley—where apricot orchards were displaced by computer makers which were in turn displaced by software companies in a venture-capital-fueled mad dash up the ladder of abstraction. If you want to rule the world from the command line, this is your Renaissance Florence. The architecture is a dead giveaway. With a few notable exceptions, the profoundly unimaginative suburban office parks are full of buildings built for people who couldn't care less because they live on the internet, meatspace being but a poor shadow of the digital dimension they can bend to their wills with a single commit.

Plagued as they are by drought and wildfire, Californians love to talk about how water is power. They talk less about how power is water. Power flows through the social hierarchies we build to channel it, eroding them along the way. Sometimes it picks up silt over thousands of cycles, depositing it into the deltas we call institutions. You can dam it up to create authority or share it with irrigation. Every once in a while an unexpected earthquake like the invention of agriculture or nuclear weapons changes the landscape abruptly, but all that power never stops flowing, it just finds a new route back to the source.

The internet was just such an earthquake. It is refactoring politics and money and romance and entertainment and work and identity and information and pretty much every other element of our social geography. As a result, power is flooding into this here valley as fast as it's losing its water. The internet is guzzling power like the Devil's Throat at Iguazu, and where power goes, I follow.

I was the Resident-at-Large: our cabal's sole field agent. My compatriots orchestrated events from our sunken headquarters, deploying me whenever a task was too sensitive to be delegated. Every architect needs a general contractor to make their vision real. That was why they'd buffed up my training in each of their respective specialties. That was why Leia was so keen to slot me in. I was what CIA had that the other Mindanao acronyms didn't: human intel, a spy on the ground.

So I drank craft beers with Palantir solution architects who were more than happy to brag about the extremely classified details of their foreign government contracts. I weaseled into forums where constitutional lawyers and network engineers traded notes on how to evade demands or incursion from NSA. I spent a weekend kite-boarding with a group of VCs investing in early stage military tech, one of whom was an Analog member. I successfully solicited an invite, but discovered nothing of interest over the fancy cocktails we consumed while playing an overly complicated board game by the roaring fire. I bluffed my way into CRISPR labs at UC Berkeley and robotics labs at Stanford. To make up for Mindanao's privations, I sipped embarrassing quantities of very expensive coffee which also happened to be very good—robbing me of what otherwise might have been a prime opportunity to roast Leia about her gourmand-infested homeland.

But my real task was Phillip.

Phillip had leveraged his love of computers to get heavy into crypto, and when he'd lost everything, managed to leverage his blockchain cred into a job at Threshold, one of the internet giants whose plush lairs encircle the San Francisco Bay—the kind of company that offers stock options and unlimited LaCroix to anyone who can make machines dream. And when I caught up with Phillip over some truly delectable Union City dosas, he let it slip that he had something special for me—confirming Leia's briefing.

Actually, Phillip didn't really have something special. He had *access* to something special. Some of his esteemed colleagues who worked on the security side of things had gotten roped into a new project in the silicon division and it was super-duper hush-hush which had, of course, piqued Phillip's curiosity and did it pique mine?

Why yes, Phillip. Consider my curiosity sufficiently piqued.

So I signed in under a fake name, donned my guest badge, piled my plate high with free lunch prepared by a chef who had started her career at Chez Panisse, sat at a table facing the exit, and waited for Phillip to arrive with the unassuming thumb drive that I would spirit away, decrypt, and hand over to Bisrat. In return, Phillip would be graced with a financial windfall into an offshore account that would enable him to substantially shorten his tenure at a firm that was treating him quite a bit better than his parents ever had. Some people just don't know when to coast, and I'm quite adept at pushing their buttons.

And then, precisely ninety-seven seconds before Phillip is supposed to waltz in, as I'm in the middle of raising a forkful of perfectly dressed *puntarelle* to my mouth,

Caroline the barista from Miami walks by the crowded door I'm watching, glances over at me, and winks.

My heart skips a beat.

The fire alarms go off.

The lights go out.

There are times when things just go your way. You hit a string of green lights on the way home from work. You win fifty dollars on a Scratcher. The hottie swipes right. Despite the dismal forecast, it doesn't rain on your picnic.

This was not one of those times.

I was a shadow among shadows—the only illumination filtered in through windows blank with fog, the kind of fog that blinds and conceals, sequestering us to fumble in perfect privacy.

23

Did you forget about her, too? Careful, Caroline slips memory's bonds as expertly as cruder handcuffs. She is a wraith in a world of golems, the panpipe in a symphony orchestra. When she is there, you cannot deny her, but the moment you turn away, she vanishes.

May the knowledge that you are not alone in your amnesia offer some small modicum of solace. I was trying to forget her, to lose myself in my tale, wrapping narrative around me like an invisibility cloak, hoping against hope that Scheherazade was real, and a story might save my skin.

Instead, I'm looking into Caroline's eyes down the barrel of a gun, and the truth I glimpse in those unnerving depths is that the thing I'm hiding from is precisely what I deserve.

No wonder I'm fleeing it so desperately.

But I'm getting ahead of myself.

Sitting there, fire alarm blaring, forkful of salad frozen halfway to my mouth, the thing I wanted more than anything was not to flee, but to *pursue*.

I wanted to dash through darkened halls, take the stairs three at a time, and burst out onto the manicured campus, lanyard flapping behind me, only to see her sprinting away through the fog toward the parking lots. I wanted to dodge the confused software engineers emerging bleary-eyed from a building that was definitely not on fire, steal a Ducati, and roar after her Tesla up 280, leaving CHP with their wailing sirens in our rubber-scented wake. I wanted to see San Francisco materialize over the horizon, evade her co-conspirators, slide the bike under the trailer of an eighteen wheeler as she shot the gaps between oncoming traffic, and parkour my way up the skyscraper as her elevator ascended, arriving just in time to step between her and the waiting helicopter, holding up a palm and shouting through the howling downwash: "Who *are* you?"

Or maybe it was all a grand coincidence and Caroline the barista from Miami had moved out to California and landed a cushy corporate gig pulling espressos for techies. But the timing. And the *wink*. I hate coincidences almost as much as I hate surprise birthday parties.

There were enough red flags for a CCP parade, but they didn't change the fact that the thing I *had* to do wasn't the thing I *wanted* to do. I wasn't a tourist. I was here for a reason. And while that reason was getting progressively more complicated, I couldn't simply charge off after an anomaly, no matter how anomalous.

So I battened down the hunter's yen, lowered my fork, and went off in search of Phillip.

24

When I finally found Phillip in the crowd milling about on the lawn, I gave him the signal that we should meet in the backup location. I didn't want to risk any of his coworkers noticing him handing me a flash drive, and I didn't trust Phillip to have the nerve or the skills to make a clean pass.

We reconvened at Rodin's Burghers of Calais sculpture in Stanford's Memorial Court. Fog this thick was unusual here, and gave the bronze figures a sense of ghostly movement, as if they might stumble onto the manicured grass, anguish blinding them to the fact they that stood in the wrong millennium on the wrong continent—lost in themselves, as we all are.

I must admit that relief flooded through me when Phillip slunk through the sandstone arch. Caroline's surprise reappearance had caught me up in an avalanche of possible scenarios and correlations. Standing here sipping on my rapidly cooling latte, mind and heart racing, I had begun to suspect that Phillip might be about to go the same way as Lorenzo and wind up a bloated corpse in the San Francisco Bay. I really, really didn't want that to happen. I didn't want to cover up another murder. I didn't want to live in a world where my agents' souls kept mysteriously vacating their owners' bodies. I didn't want my inaugural mission as a Resident-at-Large to end in a disaster that would likely end me. I didn't want to risk the shared dream we were secretly striving to realize.

But here was Phillip, not a corpse but a living, breathing man wearing jeans, desert boots, and a wool jacket with the collar popped to ward off the chill. I passed him his coffee. He frowned down at the beverage he hadn't asked for.

"Two men standing in a courtyard makes people wonder," I said. "Two men drinking coffee together makes people forget and move on. We're just over-caffeinated postdocs arguing the finer points of Rovelli's theory of quantum gravity."

Phillip nodded, took a sip. Anxiety radiated off him.

I reached out and touched the shoulder of one of the sculptures. The metal was smooth and cold.

"What the fuck happened back there?" asked Phillip.

"I was going to ask you the same thing," I said.

His face hardened. "I did everything according to plan," he said. "Get in. Get the data. Get out. And then right as I get to the cafeteria, the fire alarm goes off."

Phillip was in this for himself. And the thing about people who are in it for themselves is that when shit goes sideways, they don't have anything to hold onto except themselves. A drowning man can't throw himself a rope. So Phillip was scared, but didn't want to admit it. This whole time he'd been dreaming about Fuck You Money and it'd only now occurred to him to internalize the downside risks associated with helping someone like me.

"Take a sip," I said, indicating the coffee.

"I don't like it, any of it," he said, shaking his head.

"Take a sip," I repeated.

He looked from me to the coffee and back again.

"You poison this or something?" he asked.

"Phillip, if I wanted you dead, you wouldn't see it coming," I said. "That's a pour-over with oat milk and two tablespoons of brown sugar, just the way you like it. Now take a fucking sip."

He stared at me for a long moment, and then obliged.

"Now take a deep breath," I said.

"Fuck off," he said.

"Indulge me," I said.

He inhaled with comic exaggeration, and exhaled loudly through his nose.

"Do you know why we're here?" I asked.

"Less and less by the second," he said.

"We're here," I said, "because I put contingencies in

place. And I put contingencies in place because I'm a professional, and professionals know that no plan survives contact with reality. Now, you would never attempt to do cardiovascular surgery on yourself, would you?"

"What?" asked Phillip.

"No," I said. "You wouldn't. Because you're not a heart surgeon and you're not an idiot, so if you needed surgery, you'd look up Stanford's top expert and let her do her job. So, Phillip, let me do my job. A fire alarm going off at an inopportune moment is freaky, I get it. But this is run-of-the-mill shit for me. It's under control. I'm going to keep you safe and get you paid. Understood?"

Phillip was dithering, you could see it in his eyes. And when someone dithers, the only thing to do is still yourself. So I emulated the statues, rooting myself in place because nothing could move me and setting my will in bronze because it would not bend. I wasn't beseeching him or commanding him or threatening him. I was just communicating a basic fact, a law of nature. You couldn't argue with something that wasn't up for debate. And if you tried, you'd only shout yourself hoarse.

Of course, Phillip was right to be nervous. The operation was off-kilter. Fate was throwing me a curveball named Caroline. But the art of espionage requires convincing yourself of things you don't believe, the better to persuade others.

Phillip pinched the bridge of his nose.

"Alright," he said. "Fine."

I held my tongue.

"But I want a twenty percent bump," he continued, emboldened. "Call it danger pay."

"Out of the question," I said. "You will be paid the price we agreed on. No more, no less." The minute you agree to renegotiate a contract midway through a deal, you've implicitly undermined the other party's trust in your ability to stick to any future agreement, sabotaging the relationship.

"Do you know how much this shit is worth?" he demanded.

"To you and me, it's worth your fee," I said calmly, channeling Samantha. "You could always try to shop around for a better alternative, but if you choose that path, I can personally vouch for the fact that you will need many orders of magnitude more 'danger pay.'"

"You wouldn't…" he said.

I just let it hang there between us, keeping my expression friendly and maintaining eye contact. You can't blame a guy for testing you, but you need to make sure he's crystal clear on the results of the test.

After a moment, Phillip swallowed, then he reached into his pocket, produced a flash drive, and dropped it into my open palm.

"You made the right decision," I said, pocketing it. "I'm the kind of person you want on your softball team. Check your account in three hours. And stay sharp, there may be additional opportunities for you soon."

He stalked away through the arch and the fog swallowed him. Wealth is wanting what you have. Money is a tool for trading what you have for what you want. Both are important, but if, like Phillip, you mistake money for wealth, you will never be wealthy no matter how much money you accumulate. Phillip would lose his illicit earnings to speculation within a year. People like him always do, which is what makes them so useful to people like me.

I sipped my latte and turned to the nearest Burgher, staring up into his downcast eyes. Do you know their story? In 1346, during the Hundred Years War, England laid siege to Calais. The city held out as long as it could, but eventually starvation forced them to surrender. The king of England offered to spare the people of Calais if six of its leaders volunteered to be executed and walked out the gates with nooses around their necks and the keys to the city in their hands. The richest man in Calais volunteered, and five others with him. After they handed themselves over—certain of their impending deaths—the English queen intervened to spare them.

I reached out and ran my thumb along the sculpture's cheekbone. Having accepted the commission to commemorate them, Rodin defied his clients' wish to present these six saviors as classical champions, and instead sought to capture their profound angst as they went to meet their fate. True heroism is miserable: in any story, the hero is the one who suffers the most.

That's what people like Phillip have forgotten. And people like Phillip are the reason this great nation is sliding from hegemon to laughingstock. Self-aggrandizement blinds them to the power of self-sacrifice. You can't become a part of something greater than yourself if you don't give yourself over to it.

How do I know all this stuff about the Burghers of Calais? Or about Damocles for that matter? My abuela homeschooled us in the classics. The woman who carved through flesh and red tape to get my family out of Cuba. Americans don't realize how good they have it, so they take their country for granted, inviting its enemies to gain ground. But *we* knew. *We* remember. My abuela made sure that me and all the other great-grandkids felt it in our bones. Dystopia exists, and it's not a goddamn HBO series. America saved us—and bastions don't protect themselves.

That's why I do what I do, even if it means offering up my soul like the Burghers. And that's why I held Phillip in contempt even as I pitied him, even as I used him to defend his country. And this would have been a good day's work in its defense if it hadn't been for that wink.

25

The wink was a problem. It was a problem I had to solve. But it was a problem I had to solve after completing my mission: delivering Phillip's goods to Mindanao so that my fellow Residents could put them to work.

So I returned to my anonymous Mountain View condo, booted up my laptop, and began the process of decrypting the flash drive to verify the haul. A status bar popped up, jittering irregularly toward completion.

Silicon Valley is named for the computer chips its residents pioneered. But none of today's tech giants manufacture chips. Why bother? They can buy general-purpose semiconductors off-the-shelf, confident in the knowledge that the next generation of even faster chips is right around the corner. But then a few smarty-pants engineers realized that if they designed their own special-purpose chips and fully integrated software and hardware—like a baker growing their own wheat—they could make their computers, servers, networks, products, and services even better, faster, and more secure, establishing a new bulwark against the competition. Inevitably, the competition followed suit, and now all the big tech firms design their own custom chips and outsource the manufacturing to Taiwanese fabs.

Imagine architects drawing up plans for a skyscraper and then stepping back as builders construct it. Now imagine what sneaky fucks like me and my compadres in Mindanao might be able to do if we were to intercept the blueprints for the skyscraper. What back doors might we be able to slip through? What air ducts might we be able to infiltrate? What secret passages might we be able to insert?

You get the picture. That's why I was in California. That's why we were happy to pay Phillip the exorbitant fee he was bitching about. That was the secret I would be ferrying back to our little underground kingdom. We could use the contents of this innocuous little flash drive to unlock any chip of this design, adding vast new territories to our information empire. And once my colleagues were busy peeling back the layers of the design like an onion, I could pick up the trail of a certain rogue barista and figure out who the hell she was and what the hell she was up to.

The status bar leapt to completion and a window popped up on my screen displaying the decrypted contents.

The promised design files weren't there.

The only thing on the flash drive was a README.

Running my tongue around my suddenly dry mouth, I opened it.

"Don't panic," I read. "I couldn't just let a cute boy like you waltz off into the sunset, could I? If you need a distraction from the tsunami of crushing anxiety that is breaking over you right now, just picture me naked. Then chill the fuck out. This shouldn't take me more than a few hours. You'll have what you need faster than you can drink a cortado."

26

There are no words in the English language that will make me panic faster than "don't panic." It's like saying "don't think about bubblegum-flavored condoms." Anyone who tells you not to panic knows that right now happens to be the perfect time for you to panic, and they almost always have a vested interest in you remaining calm, and quite often they are the source of whatever is causing you to panic in the first place. So I say: fuck 'em. Panic all you want. You have my blessing on the condition that after you finish panicking, you seek revenge. If you play your cards right, one day you'll have the oh-so-sweet pleasure of blithely telling them, "Don't panic."

I closed my laptop and took a shaky breath. The generic

faces in the generic art on the walls of this generic condo in this generic neighborhood leered at me as if they wanted to leach my soul to slake their bitter soullessness.

Was Phillip in on this? Did he know he was selling me hot air? Had he been playing at being difficult in order to bolster my trust in a faulty product? Was he a double agent playing both sides and trying to collect as many chips as he could before he got thrown out of the casino? No. Conscience wouldn't have stopped him from pursuing such a course of action, but I didn't think he had it in him. He might be a selfish jerk, but either he was a selfish jerk who believed his goods were genuine, or he was a better actor than I was willing to give him credit for.

Then, what? Had the barista somehow managed to hack the system such that she was able to intercept the design files as Phillip was downloading them onto the flash drive and replace them with her README? That seemed complex to the point of baroque, a scheme that Occam's razor would slice to tattered shreds.

I replayed the scene in my mind. Swallowing a bite of crunchy *puntarelle*. People bustling around the entrance to the cafeteria. A familiar face glimpsed over a shoulder. The wink. *Puntarelle*. Crowd. Wink. *Puntarelle*. Crowd. Wink. Yes, she could have simply pickpocketed Phillip. It would have been easy enough to jostle him in the hallway, especially if you happened to be an attractive woman who knew what she was doing, all the more so in the chaotic exodus of a fire alarm.

But I was getting sidetracked. Attribution didn't matter.

At least, not yet. The important part wasn't figuring out how I had gotten into this situation, but how I was going to get out of it.

I could go back to Phillip and demand he try again. We'd have no choice but to up the budget, but dollars were trivial. On the other hand, he might balk. Even if he went for it, he'd know something had gone wrong on our end—and that wasn't a good look.

I could hunt down Caroline, figure out her angle, and recover the drive, if she had, in fact, stolen it. I'd return to Mindanao victorious, even if it wasn't the victory we'd been seeking. But a fleeting glimpse of someone in a crowded building didn't offer many clues to follow up on, and in the meantime, it wouldn't take long for the other Residents to start asking where the precious chip designs were.

I could report everything to Leia. The Residents would tear the world apart to figure out what had happened and who Caroline really was. Then we could decide whether it was worth going back to Phillip or whether we should tap a different source to get what we needed. But to explain the contents of the README and the implications of the wink, I'd need to tell Leia about my one-night stand with Caroline in Miami, a fling that I'd conveniently neglected to mention in my report on Lorenzo. She and, by extension, the Residents would determine that I was unreliable and, at best, I'd lose my job. At worst, well, the Mindanao operation was sensitive enough that my replacement's first assignment would likely be to eliminate any outstanding risks of exposure: namely, me. If I'd established more of a track record, things might play out differently, but this was my first op in this new role, my last op had ended in the Miami City Cemetery, and there were so many factions involved with Mindanao, none of them forgiving.

If I told the truth, I was toast. But it was hard to imagine a lie convincing enough to cover my extremely bare ass.

I realized I'd been pacing in tight circles around the living room. I stopped by the galley kitchen and pressed my forehead down on the granite countertop, trying to ground myself, to slow my racing mind.

Think.

Think.

Think.

I poured a glass of water. Gulped it down. Poured another. Stared at the tiny bubbles trapped against the inside of the glass. Refraction warped and enlarged my fingers in the background on the other side. Water sloshed in my belly, and I felt suddenly empty, a living shell, a sea cave filled and drained by fickle tides.

I couldn't hide the fact that I didn't have the chip designs. And I couldn't lie to Leia about something like this. If I did, I'd be more selfish than Phillip. Instead of sacrificing myself for my people, like the Burghers, I'd be sacrificing the best interests of my people for myself.

Fuck. Why hadn't I just reported my one-night stand in Miami? If I had, this would have been bad but not irreparable. I was getting sloppy, and for someone in my line of work, sloppiness is fatal.

I slammed the glass down onto the counter. It shattered, sending shards skittering away and water spilling into the sink and onto the floor.

Fuck.

This was just so *stupid*. Like a soldier in the trenches dying from an infection because he cut himself shaving. Such a pointless trap to have caught myself in.

But I was here now. And if I was honest with myself, there was only one thing I could do. I stared down at the laptop on the coffee table. It looked so innocuous just sitting there. But the minute I placed a secure call to Leia and explained what had happened, all hell would break loose. That little machine would carry the signal of my demise as easily as a tweet, packets zipping through network arterioles to seal my fate.

I sat down on the couch and opened the laptop. The screen glowed to life, asking for my password. My palms were sweating. My mouth felt dry and fuzzy despite the water I'd just chugged. Honesty is overrated. Steeling myself, I entered the password and–

The doorbell rang.

I looked up. I wasn't expecting any visitors. And who even knew this was where I was staying?

I set down the laptop. There was a chef's knife in the kitchen and an emergency sidearm in the bedside-table drawer. I hadn't expected to need serious firepower here, so that was it. Activated by the doorbell, a screen by the apartment door piped in video from the building's entrance.

I hurried over, cataloguing possible escape routes.

But nobody was staring back at me through the camera.

The only thing visible on the landing was an enormous fruit basket.

27

Odysseus ended the decade-long Trojan War by offering his adversaries a gift: a giant wooden horse that they wheeled into their besieged city without noticing the Greek commandos hidden in its belly who snuck out in the dead of night to open the gates of Troy and rain destruction. This is exactly the kind of bedtime story my abuela would read us in kindergarten—no Winnie-the-Pooh in our realpolitik household. Staring at the generously provisioned fruit basket on the screen by my apartment door, I could not dislodge the moral of that particular tale: gifts were traps.

Avoiding lines of sight to my apartment's windows, I snatched my laptop from the coffee table, set it up on the kitchen counter, and opened the building's security camera feeds, which I'd hacked first thing when I moved in a few weeks ago. I clicked around and found angles on the landing. The basket was overflowing with apples, olive oil, pomegranates, marmalade, persimmons, kettle corn, guavas, tulips, and chocolate. A plush bald eagle sat at a jaunty angle in the middle of the basket like a dragon atop its hoard.

I scanned views from the other exterior cameras. A van disappeared around the corner onto the next street. Beyond that, I couldn't see anyone else, though there was plenty of cover if a team was waiting to take me when I opened the front door.

Scrolling the feeds back in time, I watched a single delivery van double-park in front of the building. A uniformed driver emerged, retrieved the gift basket, deposited it on the landing, double checked his tablet, rang my doorbell, and drove away. I clicked through the other cameras.

Nothing.

Retreating to the bedroom, I stuck the handgun in the back of my jeans where my t-shirt draped over it and retrieved the black pelican case from the closet. Crouching to the side of the apartment door, I unbolted it, cracked it open, and waited.

Silence.

I used a tactical periscope to check the hall.

Empty.

I counted to ten, then stepped out, locking the door behind me. One, two, three flights of stairs and I was at the utility door to the roof. Using the periscope to make sure the area was clear, I propped open the door with the pelican case and released the drone from its foam embrace.

I flew it straight up, looking for movement on adjacent rooftops where waiting snipers would be spooked by its whine. But the surrounding rooftops were empty. I queued up an automatic search pattern and it swooped in long intersecting arcs that expanded around the building, checking all vehicles and windows with a vantage on my apartment. But to all appearances, this was just another day in suburbia. Finally, I spiraled the drone in on the fruit basket, inspecting it from all angles and extending a scalpel-tipped probe to pierce the transparent plastic wrapping and confirm that the bananas were, in fact, bananas.

I sat there for a moment on the stairs, gun digging into my lower back. Maybe there was some kind of lightweight explosive device rigged in the base of the basket. Or maybe the pomegranates were poisoned. Or maybe the handle would register my touch and release a cloud of noxious gas. Nobody should know where this apartment is, nobody except my fellow Residents, who wouldn't send me unsolicited gifts. Should I grab my go-bag and disappear, taking careful measures to evade anyone tailing me, and make my way back to Mindanao to confess and face my fate?

Recalling the drone, I took the stairs down two at a time.

I wasn't going to end my career fleeing a pile of seasonal produce.

Throwing a quick glance up and down the street, I snatched up the basket, hurried back to my apartment, and tore it apart.

It wasn't a bomb.

It wasn't booby-trapped with a gas canister.

It was a goddamn fruit basket.

I guess the pomegranates could have been poisoned, but I didn't taste one to find out.

It took a minute for me to realize that the plush eagle was a puppet, and that secreted in a finger of the puppet's glove was a tiny present expertly wrapped in bright orange tissue paper, complete with a tiny card.

I ripped open the package.

Inside was a flash drive.

"See?" read the card. "I promised you'd get what you needed. I do hope you didn't panic. I asked them to include a stress ball, but they said they were all out—apparently it's annual review season in the Valley."

28

The trouble was the flash drive had exactly what I needed. If the drive had instead been loaded with juicy kompromat and a threat of blackmail, or even if the contents had been obviously doctored, I would have had no choice but to come clean to Leia and the Residents. My path forward would have been arduous—and likely short—but clear. But this crown jewel of the fruit basket contained the exact chip designs I had commissioned Phillip to steal.

My mission was a success.

At least, as long as you ignored the little... detour.

And nobody else *knew* about the detour, yet.

The Mindanao facility still smelled like lavender, which, as caves go, was a hell of a lot better than batshit. Home, sweet home.

Bisrat was reverse engineering the chip designs, tasking remote teams with subcomponents, unraveling embedded systems, flagging opportunities for manipulation, and generally being a sorceress—her pod was a flying carpet she piloted through the dense megalopolis of silicon architecture.

Jerry was navigating an equally intricate maze of political implications, how we could use this as leverage with whom, what trade and tax and quota deals were on the line, what scope of information we might hope to glean from the access Bisrat was working to engineer, and how we could trade up that information to further American interests.

Samantha was... actually, I had no idea what Samantha was doing. Probably dreaming up innovative ways to murder people or overseeing a strike team taking out a terrorist cell or something. That's what special ops weirdos do, right?

(If you tell Samantha I called her a weirdo, I will hunt you down and kill you with my bare hands. She taught me how.)

I had delivered the goods, and the other Residents were putting those goods to work, which left me... microwaving pad thai and retreating to my pod to stare out across my digital desert at the lengthening shadows of Joshua Trees.

I had to tell them. At a bare minimum, I had to tell Leia. I didn't know who Caroline was. I didn't know how she'd intercepted the flash drive, what she'd done with it, or why she'd returned it. I didn't know how she knew where my apartment was, or the reason she'd revealed herself to me at the cafeteria. I didn't know what she'd been doing in Miami.

Come to think of it, the only thing I *did* know was that I needed to report her. Caroline might have doctored the designs. She almost certainly would have made a copy for herself. I couldn't let my colleagues act on intel that might be tainted. I had to tell Leia. I had to tell her everything. From the cortado to the fruit basket. I had broken protocol. Like a newbie. Like an *idiot*. There would be consequences, hopefully manageable, possibly fatal.

"Congratulations."

I dropped my fork and lukewarm pad thai spilled on my lap.

"Fuck, Leia," I said. "Can't you ring or something before appearing like a goddamn genie?"

Leia was sitting on a lump of granite, bathed in evening light. I imagined the meatspace office she was beaming in from, the intervening machines transmuting her ergonomic chair into geology and casting the virtual sunset across her face.

"Time to debrief," she said.

"And you couldn't wait for me to finish my dinner?" I demanded.

She raised her eyebrows.

I sighed.

A beat.

I used a napkin to scoop up the fallen noodles.

Another beat.

"Leia," I said. "There's something I need to tell you."

"Speak, wunderkind," said Leia.

There are rare moments when the fates pause in their machinations to cast their gaze your way, nodes where many lives intersect, choices that will braid them together, or tear them apart.

I was a flipping coin, a rolling die.

It was intoxicating and excruciating.

It was intolerable.

"Remember when I tasted your kombucha?" I asked.

She raised her eyebrows. "I believe you described it as 'unicorn semen.'"

"The coffee here is worse," I said.

I told myself this wasn't the right time, knowing full well that those who tell themselves that particular lie so often discover that the right time never comes.

29

While my colleagues deconstructed, refactored, and exploited the stolen chip designs, I set to work tracking down Caroline.

This was a delicate operation. I didn't want any of the other Residents to get suspicious, so I worked exclusively from my pod. Thankfully, most of the others did, too, and it was normal to be cagey with each other about our work because so much of it was either need-to-know or specific enough to our respective disciplines to be mutually incomprehensible.

This gave me cover to spend hours at a time scouring memory and the vast pools of data at my disposal to pick up Caroline's scent. I sketched her face, letting the computer make thousands of small tweaks that I would respond to, iterating toward an ever-closer match in a game of algorithmic hot-and-cold. I read Yelp reviews of the Miami coffeeshop, scanning through photos customers had posted of the latte art. I replayed the night we'd spent together over and over again in my head, trying to dredge up any identifying details. I indexed every company that delivered fruit baskets in my Bay Area apartment's zip code. I cross-referenced every location I had seen her. I extrapolated elaborate fantasias of means and motive. Feeling like a Hollywood spy crawling through air-ducts into the heart of a secret facility—assumedly the architects of such facilities never anticipate such a possibility, despite the preponderance of evidence served up by summer blockbusters—I burrowed up the thread of fiber that Bisrat's colleagues had spliced into Threshold's trunk line and sifted through their campus camera feeds.

I was afraid, despite the blister I'd acquired burning her tiny card, that Caroline was, in fact, a ghost, a fragment of my paranoid imagination or, worse, a living, breathing human being who was inexplicably but totally absent from the buzzing tangle of the internet. Such an absence would imply vast resources, resources that would be impossible for me to counter without looping in Leia and the Residents, which was getting less appealing by the second.

If I could find Caroline, I could trap her.

I was terrified of finding nothing.

What I found was even worse: everything.

30

Caroline was a prep school kid from Massachusetts who'd followed the guardrails straight to Harvard and then on to strategy consulting. She lived in the Center of the World, the liminal intersection of Tokyo, New York City, Berlin, Singapore, London, Shanghai, Bangalore, and the internet. She only slept in first class cabins at thirty thousand feet, elevated spreadsheets into poetry, and could topple national economies with a whisper into the ear of the right magnate. A chess master had once beaten her and made the mistake of bragging about it to a niche blog. It wasn't until every major tournament banned him for arbitrary administrative reasons and his career was in shambles that he realized he'd been playing the wrong game.

The problem was that Caroline was also a surf brat raised in a middle-class Cape Town suburb who'd won regional long-boarding championships while earning her post-doc in materials science. Despite offers from leading labs, she'd left academia to co-found a carbon capture startup that the Gates Foundation placed a massive bet on. Now her ingenious machines were sucking CO_2 out of the atmosphere at two hundred facilities across sub-Saharan Africa. Along the way she'd picked up a stay-at-home husband and they'd produced three surf brats of their own.

In addition to that, Caroline was an orphan who'd carefully arranged to slip through the cracks of the Dutch social welfare system so that she could raise herself in Amsterdam's vibrant underworld, graduating from slinging pills to Euro Trippers to being the go-to fixer for international criminal syndicates looking to establish a foothold in the EU. She was rumored to have slept with the sitting queen and had singlehandedly fomented a network of literary salons that would have made Enlightenment-era Parisians sick with jealousy.

The more I looked, the more I found. Caroline didn't just contain multitudes, multitudes contained Caroline. Thousands of social media accounts purported to represent her. Her face appeared in countless photos that had supposedly been taken at the same time but in different places. Her identities spawned new identities that simultaneously cross-referenced and contradicted each other. She was a kindergarten teacher, an investment banker, a stylist, a ministry staffer, a journalist, and a sex worker. She was married, single, divorced, widowed, and dating. She had a podcast and a tumor and a gorilla. There was a YouTube video of her landing a triple axel on a frozen lake in Siberia and a GitHub repo where she'd authored a popular open-source project. Pistachio, chocolate, butternut crunch, and red bean were each her favorite ice cream.

Caroline wasn't a person.

She was a fractal.

No matter where I aimed the all-seeing eye my masters had so generously bestowed upon me, there was Caroline staring back at me from the digital abyss.

31

"Knock, knock."

Buy time. "Who's there?" I asked.

"Samantha."

Fuck. I desperately shuffled away the constellation of data points surrounding me, my pod a lone starship wandering a galaxy of Carolines. "Samantha who?"

"Samantha, jackass. Open up."

Glancing around to double check that Joshua Tree was free of incriminating evidence, I opened the door. "Did your ancestors make a name for themselves in donkey husbandry?"

She blinked. "That's not my *surname*, that's—Do you have anything else to say, or would you like those to be your last words?"

Anger makes for effective deflection, but take it too far and you raise a different sort of question entirely, not an appealing prospect when your interlocutor could end your life seventeen different ways using only her left pinkie.

"To what do I owe the pleasure of your company?" I asked.

"Team meeting," she said. "Stat. Move yourself, shitsicle."

"Thank heaven for the AC," I said, grateful for the excuse to follow her down the corridor and away from the sucking maw of my research. "You wouldn't want me to melt."

I already told you: bad jokes are my defense mechanism.

"I'm gonna pay extra to inscribe 'melting shitsicle' on your headstone," she said.

"'Badass,'" I said thoughtfully as we arrived at the conference room. "That would be a more appropriate surname for your esteemed lineage. Samantha Badass."

That made her pause. "I don't hate it," she said grudgingly.

"The highest praise I've ever heard grace your lips."

"Don't get used to it," she said over her shoulder as she entered.

"I wouldn't dare," I said, and followed.

32

Samantha and I joined the other Residents at the semicircular conference table, which was currently perched atop Half Dome and commanded a spectacular view of Yosemite Valley.

"Good, everyone's accounted for," said Jerry. His calm felt forced.

"Do you think they realize how disruptive this is?" said Bisrat. "It takes hours for me to get into the right head-space to ID potential exploits in designs this complex. Like untangling a knot the size of a small moon."

"People who manage people live on calendar time," said Jerry. "People who solve problems live outside time, at least temporarily. When people who manage people who solve problems forget that interruption is sabotage, things fall apart."

"Auditioning for house guru?" asked Samantha, but Jerry just smiled his maddeningly benign smile.

"So," I said, trying and failing to banish afterimages of innumerable Carolines from my mind's eye. "Why are we here?"

An awkward exchange of glances.

"OK," I said. "None of us knows. Great. Another meeting without an agenda."

I played that line as if it were a continuation of Bisrat and Jerry's banter about how annoying meetings can be, and the group seemed to buy it—they piled on with complaints of their own. But while they bitched, my insides set like fresh concrete under summer sun. It was possible nobody had sent us an agenda out of pure managerial incompetence. That was the most likely situation given that banal incompetence is the root of all evil, and seemingly ubiquitous at our blessed employer. But when someone neglects to send you an agenda, sometimes that means *you* are the agenda. And I did not want to be the agenda. Not one little bit. There were ghosts in the machine, and I needed to bust them before I got busted.

Condensation beaded on the glass of water in front of me. If I shattered it on the edge of the table, I'd have a makeshift weapon. Would Samantha have allowed it to be placed there if she knew she might need to subdue me? She was the one who had so recently taught me to evaluate the killing potential of any object within reach. On the other hand, maybe she thought I'd notice something was off if the water wasn't there. Or she knew she could disable me in under five seconds no matter what I might be able to get my hands on. I know you think the world of me, but even I have relative incompetencies, and me vs. Samantha in hand-to-hand combat would be like the Pillsbury Doughboy attempting to take on Darth Vader.

The group's catalog of minor grievances ceased abruptly, yanking me out of my spiral. We weren't alone atop Half Dome anymore. Our physical table now extended seamlessly into a digital half that completed the circle. And facing us on the other side were our bosses.

Leia smiled her sharkiest smile, and I knew I was chum.

"We're on," she said. "Green light, motherfuckers."

33 ≡≡≡≡≡

≡≡≡≡≡ **That phone in your pocket,** that watch on your wrist, that car in your driveway, that pacemaker in your abuela's chest, all of them depend on semiconductors: the silicon minds that enable machine cognition. We live our lives wrapped in software cocoons, but ubiquity confers invisibility, and when you drop that hot new meme into a thread with your besties, you probably aren't giving much thought to the itty-bitty logic gates opening and closing to enable all those emoji laden reactions.

The more logic gates, the more powerful the chip, so engineers have done their level best to bend the laws of physics in service of cramming as many of the little buggers as close together as possible. They've gotten quite good at it.

Computing power has increased more than a trillion-fold over the past seventy years, and now they can fit fifty billion transistors onto a chip the size of a fingernail.

This is... not easy. Arguably, semiconductor manufacturing requires more scientific and technical expertise than any other industry. An engineer once described the challenge as equivalent to shooting an arrow from your backyard to hit an apple on the surface of the moon. Feel free to dream up your own wacky metaphor, but regardless, it makes rocket science look like child's play: the computer that took the Apollo astronauts to the moon was only twice as powerful as a Nintendo—like, not even a *Super* Nintendo, let alone an iPhone.

So how do you squeeze that many teeny tiny transistors onto a silicon wafer? Robots draw them on the chip with lasers. Yes, you heard me right. Modern civilization is built on the backs of laser-wielding robots. But the robots can't use just any old lasers, because transistors are now so minuscule that they're actually smaller than the wavelength of any naturally occurring visible light, so using normal light to draw them would be like trying to illustrate the intricate geometry of a fern frond with an oversized Sharpie highlighter.

At this point, if I was in charge, I would have thrown up my hands and said, "You know what, I think the computers we've got are fast enough. Well done, everyone—and three cheers for the laser-wielding robots."

This defeatist attitude is why nobody would ever put me in charge of semiconductor manufacturing. Instead, the people *actually* in charge dedicated seventeen years and billions upon billions of dollars to inventing a process that puts centuries of alchemical pursuit of the philosopher's stone to shame.

Ready for the recipe? (Do not try this at home.)

Shoot a droplet of molten tin into a vacuum.

Hit the falling droplet with a laser that flattens it into a falling pancake.

Hit the falling pancake with a more powerful laser that vaporizes it into plasma, releasing extreme ultraviolet light with a wavelength so short it can only survive in outer space.

Use special mirrors polished to a smoothness of less than one atom's thickness to bounce the light onto a reticle that reflects the pattern of the chip's design.

Use more mirrors to shrink the reticle pattern and draw it on the exposed silicon wafer.

Repeat fifty thousand times a second with perfect accuracy.

Clever as fuck, if you ask me.

And there is only one team on our pale blue dot of a planet who can pull off this miraculous feat, which is why Leia shipped me off to the coastal swamp also known as the Netherlands.

34

I stared out the window as the plane descended into Schiphol.

My first glimpse of Amsterdam was a diffuse glow against the dark. As we approached, the glow broadened and sharpened and splintered into countless discrete lights. Empty office buildings. Streetlamps. Hotel rooftops. Dining room windows. Cars humming along highways. Boats floating down canals. Each firefly pinprick of illumination had its own backstory, its own purpose, its own part to play in humanity's sprawling drama.

I like flying. The uncomfortable seats. The silly rules. The monotonous routine. There's something about being tens of thousands of feet above the surface of the Earth that enforces a kind of stasis. It's those science-fiction stories where astronauts travel between the stars in suspended animation. There's real life. Your friends, family, work, dreams, fears, chores, habits, and issues. And then there's flying on a passenger jet. Seatbelts, oxygen masks, terrible food, B-list movies, and the inevitable screaming baby. Whatever air travel is, it's not real life. It's hitting pause in a video game. All your problems are *down there*. You've been temporarily plucked out of your otherwise inescapable context. You can take a breath of stale air. You can let your mind hover, if not wander. Sometimes you can even recontextualize the problems *down there* before being unceremoniously shoved back into them.

The lights stretched nearly to the horizon, an urban network diagram. Somehow, it was impossible to define the edges of the city. I tried to outline it in my mind's eye, but I couldn't tell where the city ended and the suburbs began, or where the suburbs gave way to countryside. Nothing stood alone. Everything bled into everything else. Any lines I drew would be impositions, not observations.

The flight attendants reminded us to fasten our seatbelts, stow our tray tables, and return our seats to their upright and locked positions. The man seated next to me gripped the armrest, knuckles white. I told him a bad joke to diffuse his anxiety. He laughed nervously, and his grip relaxed a bit, so I told him another one.

The wheels deployed with a clunk. The swirl of lights rushed up to envelop us. The world took on texture and depth and detail. I could see an ambulance cruising up a side road, an aircraft marshaller waving glowing orange batons, a child staring at us from the brightly lit terminal.

Touchdown.

35

An evening breeze ruffled the surface of the canal, blowing intricate whorls across the water, the fading ruby-gold light touching up reality like an Instagram filter.

As I waited for Barend, I tried and mostly failed to take a moment to enjoy the view from his veranda. I needed to marshal my resources. I needed to bend the will of one foreign power to frustrate the will of another.

Just another day at the office.

Back in the conference room on Mindanao, a bead of sweat sliding down my butt crack, I'd thought Leia had found me out. Surely, she'd seen through my thin veneer of competence to the miserable wretch beneath—a shadowy parade of Carolines stretching out behind me. But no.

The alpha predator didn't gobble me up. Quite the opposite. The tainted goods I'd delivered were the ammunition she needed to stalk her prey.

You could see it in the set of her posture, and in how the other bosses deferred to her during the meeting. Only a few months before, I'd been a newcomer to Mindanao, and Leia had been just another member of the cabal directing Operation Glass Ceiling. I don't know what kind of horses she traded to get a seat at the table and her man in the mix, but they must have been thoroughbreds capable of sweeping the Kentucky Derby. And I had delivered. Whatever Beltway game Leia was running, Phillip's pilfered chip designs had strengthened her hand to the extent that her besuited NSA, DoD, and State equivalents were content to let her take charge, or, if not content, at least unwilling to oppose her—the best any despot can hope for.

You'd think Leia's inexorable ascent through the DC hierarchy would make me swoon with self-satisfaction. I'd chosen the right patron, given her what she wanted, and now I was drafting her like a doped cyclist on the last leg of the Tour de France. Except that Leia's waxing ambition terrified me, not least because it rendered my own absolution all but impossible: the faster she pedaled, the less I wanted to admit that I hadn't checked her brakes.

So now I was pedaling my heart out just to keep up.

Win or die, motherfuckers.

"Do you take cream with your coffee?" my host, Barend, called from the kitchen. His mild accent rendered the everyday words exotic. I returned to myself, sitting on the veranda watching lights come on in the houses on the opposite bank as dusk deepened. If the Netherlands is a swamp, Barend is its swamp monster.

36

"**Wow, Barend. Wow.** I would commit war crimes for your *appeltaart*," I said. "And not just any war crimes. Like, the really nasty ones. The International Criminal Court would ask why I perpetrated such atrocities, and I'd say, 'It was the only way I could get one more slice.'"

Barend's eyes crinkled when he smiled. "The baker at the Winkel Café in Jordaan shared the recipe, and I've made a few tweaks to it over the years," he said, reaching over to dollop more fresh whipped cream onto my plate. "The trick is choosing the right apples. You want really tart ones, otherwise it just tastes sweet instead of tasting like apples."

I washed down the rich pastry with a sip of coffee (dark roast, French press, black). "You know why I'm here, right? Aside from taking the opportunity to taste your fabulous cooking."

The smile stayed on his face, but left his eyes. "I haven't the faintest clue."

"Surely you can hazard a guess," I said.

"Far be it from me to read America's mind," he said.

"I'm not sure America is of a single mind about anything," I said. "But her government has some very specific dreams that you can ensure come true."

"All in the service of freedom," said Barend.

"And democracy and progress and equality and all the rest," I said. When people get sarcastic about principles, the only move is to muscle in with earnestness and let them draw their own conclusions as to the intended level of irony. "The Stars and Stripes don't fly for anything less."

Barend snorted.

Barend is a middle manager in the Dutch agency responsible for sports. Officially, he's in charge of drafting doomed proposals for the Netherlands to host the next Olympics and making sure that Dutch youngsters have appropriate access to pickleball courts. Unofficially, Barend is the ultimate Dutch fixer. Like Robert Moses orchestrating a renovation of New York City from the unlikely chair of parks commissioner, Barend directs Dutch policy from a desk surrounded by deflated soccer balls. He writes speeches for the prime minister. He goes to raves with the queen. Everyone owes him a favor. Everyone solicits his advice. He is unthreatening enough to be a real threat. Oh, and he brews a mean cup of coffee.

I took another sip.

Barend is not a dummy.

Barend knew why I was there.

Have you ever heard of ASML? The most valuable technology company in Europe? The people who build the laser-wielding robots that make semiconductors? You can't make a modern civilization without advanced chips, and you can't make advanced chips without ASML lithography machines, so every Great Power or aspiring Great Power in the world is desperate to acquire the technology and deny it to their peers. As a result, ASML has itself become a chip in the Great Game, and aging Uncle Sam, incarnated in yours truly, will do whatever it takes to keep these treasures from rising China, whose agents have somehow convinced Barend to pull whatever strings are required to approve exporting them to Chinese fabs. Right now, China is still a decade behind the cutting edge of semiconductor manufacturing, but gaining access to ASML wizardry would put them on the fast track to success. Operation Glass Ceiling won't let that happen, hence me gobbling Barend's appeltaart.

I leaned forward and stabbed my fork into the pastry. "You should be more circumspect with your recipes than the Winkel."

Barend tsked. "They are *our* recipes," he said. "We will do whatever we like with them."

"Of course you will," I said, leaning back again. "Far be it from me to read Holland's mind."

"We are a complex people," he said, smiling his tight

little smile.

"Aren't we all?" I said. "On an entirely unrelated note, I just received some very disappointing news."

"Oh?"

"It seems that Shell contractors working on the Saih Rawl concession in Oman were involved in the Baluchi pogrom," I said apologetically. "Extremely fucked up— like ICC-level nasty. Not something the royals would want surfacing in the news cycle. Naturally, I can't imagine they were committing war crimes for a slice of your appeltaart..."

Barend's silence spoke volumes.

37

I decided to walk back to my hotel to give myself time to gather my thoughts. Fireflies danced over the canal, and streetlights illuminated the tastefully renovated facades of centuries old Dutch townhomes. The village felt earnest and kind and domestic in a way that made me feel like a dangerous and unwelcome interloper. It made me want to be a part of it, and that desire highlighted the extent to which I wasn't.

I am an interloper everywhere and always.

I belong only where I don't.

That's what it means to be a spy.

If you've ever been an outcast—from a foursquare tournament, a popular clique, an exclusive club—then you know it gives you a special vantage from which to observe insiders. They're so caught up in themselves that they struggle to discern what's obvious to you. And it was obvious to me that Barend wanted to be convinced. He wanted to be wooed. He'd let Beijing's agents buy his patronage because it made him feel important, and my threats had made him feel even more important. Whoever made him feel most important, whoever confirmed his abundant sense of self, controlled access to ASML.

The implications made my neck tingle.

Without the oh-so-special laser-wielding robots, Chinese fabs would have to walk, not run, to the vertiginous frontier of chip manufacturing, and the good old US-of-A could continue to enjoy the benefits of technological pre-eminence for a while longer. Not that we had been resting on our laurels or anything like that... but what is a lead, if not something to squander? Shanking your opponent in the spirit of healthy competition: when the world's your stage, all play is fair. The thing was–

Hold on.

The tingles were still there.

And no, I wasn't streaming an eggshell crushing video.

With great effort, I did *not* look over my shoulder.

Everything was exactly as before: windows glowing with cheery light, warm breeze off the canal, a lingering scent of jasmine.

In a word: idyllic.

I don't trust utopias. Nobody sets out to build a dystopia. Instead, people set out to build a utopia, and those who adhere strictly to the utopian plan unintentionally succeed in building a dystopia. The key word is "strictly": every plan shatters on contact with reality, so if you stick to the plan instead of adapting to reality, you end up with a broken system.

Yeah, something was definitely wrong.

Time for me to adapt to reality.

38

I cut into an alley that ran behind the line of townhomes, picked one at random, vaulted over the low fence into a side yard, and hustled past the garbage bins onto the next street.

Not too fast. Until I had a better guess as to what was going on, I shouldn't expend all my energy on a sprint, and anyway, my wingtip Oxfords weren't designed for maximum traction on cobblestones. You don't see it in spy movies, but nothing fucks up an escape like a broken ankle.

A medieval church rose dark against the stars on my right as the road curved around to the square. I strained to listen over my jack-hammering heart, but a siren blared in the distance, blocking any sounds that might indicate a tail.

This was the problem operating as a lone wolf. Wolves thrive in packs, and spies thrive in teams. Well, to be fair, we're egomaniacal enough that maybe "team" is the wrong word, but we *definitely* thrive with backup. Shit goes sideways, call in the cavalry. But when, like me, you've been deputized into what is effectively a state-sanctioned terrorist cell in which you're the only field agent, you have no choice but to figure out how to fly solo.

And no, I obviously hadn't brought a weapon to a pastry tasting on Barend's veranda, so here I was, fleeing a stalker through the tidy streets of a bucolic Dutch village.

I passed in front of the church, cut around the far corner, slipped into the deep shadow behind a buttress, and, despite my burning lungs, slowed my breathing.

Footsteps, approaching.

I did not exist. I was the cold stone pressing against my back. I was the balmy evening breeze. I was the star peeking through the black velvet haze, the owl hooting from over by the canal. I was nothing more or less than a spirit of the night.

A bulky figure hurried into view and stopped just six feet away, peering down the empty street. Damn. The buttress had granted me a moment of reprieve, but as soon as he glanced around after his quarry and looked directly at me, I was toast.

I had three seconds.

Maybe.

I could sprint off in a new direction and hope to beat him in a footrace. Of course, that assumed he didn't have a long-range weapon. I could challenge him and demand to know why he was following me, but what would Samantha think if I squandered my hard-earned opportunity to surprise him?

Damn. Damn. Damn. Damn. Damn.

Pushing off the wall, I lunged forward and kicked the side of his knee, the impact ricocheting back up through my bones. I had meant to break the joint, but he managed to twist away just in time to bend his leg and absorb some of the force of the kick. He continued the twist, spinning around to throw a punch that I just barely managed to duck, and then time ceased ticking forward and the universe spiraled down into a single unfolding instant of blurred motion, give and take, strike and block and dodge, and then, pain...

He slammed me back into the stone wall, knocking the air out of me, and then his hand was at my throat, and a savage hunger rose in his pale blue eyes, and moonlight flashed off a blade in his hand, and I thought of my abuela, and tasted her thick sweet cortado, and pined for the rush of escapist joy me and my cousins felt whenever she read to us from the *Iliad*, and–

Someone came around the buttress at a full sprint and planted their shoulder in knife dude's kidney. He staggered back and I slumped to the cobbles, lungs sucking for air. As my starry vision began to clear, I watched my attacker grappling with his attacker and, to my horror, winning.

Knife dude straddled the stranger, pinning their arms down with his knees. With every cell in my body screaming for oxygen, I forced myself up and stumbled up behind them and locked my arm around knife dude's neck, wrenching him back. This gave his other victim enough space to smash a knee into his testicles and I tightened my elbow and tried to avoid his flailing arms as his body jerked against me.

And then the other person wriggled out, popped up like a gymnast, and kicked him in the face. His body went limp, and I let him fall so as not to get dragged down on top of him.

My rescuer and I stood facing each other, gasping.

"Hi," said Caroline.

"Hi," I said.

Tires squealed on pavement as a white van shuddered to a stop beside us. The side door slid open, and before I had time to react, three men had yanked both the body and Caroline inside.

"Don't worry," she said, glancing back. "They're with me."

This was the cavalry I couldn't call.

The van rocketed off into the night.

I stood there, panting, and, not for the first time, doubting my sanity. I leaned against the church wall for support. In the distance, the owl hooted again. As if in response, I puked *appeltaart*. Sickly sweet acid corroded my throat. This made no sense. It shouldn't be happening. If I didn't hurt all over, I would have wondered whether my overactive imagination had invented the whole episode.

39

Sadly, things did not immediately start making sense.

It would have been far more convenient if they had. Reality can be stubbornly inconvenient sometimes. Frankly, it's rude. I mean, we're all part of reality, right? So why does it insist on generating all this internal tension? Why not simply allow for straightforward resolution? Does a puzzle really enjoy being separated into pieces?

But instead of the parts coming together to form a whole greater than their sum, they persisted in remaining a jumbled mess. And the mess just kept growing and growing. Needless to say, my abuela would *not* have approved.

It was easier not to report the assault than to attempt to explain its unusual conclusion. So I wrote up the meeting with Barend and kept my mouth shut about the rest and told funny jokes in decidedly bad taste and nodded in grim satisfaction when Jerry's people reported that the Netherlands had upheld their ban on exporting ASML tech to China. Oh, and, of course, I consumed too much caffeine and lost sleep plumbing the digital depths in pursuit of Caroline's proliferating ghosts.

But I didn't get to spend much time hibernating in my pod. Momentum was building. There were no more salsa parties among us Residents. Everyone was busy. Everyone was serious. Everyone kept getting busier and busier and more and more serious.

I'd share the details, but honestly it was hard to keep track because Leia et al had me zigzagging around the world like a meth-addled water strider. I intercepted rare earth smugglers in the Gulf of Aden, solicited trade secrets from a cryptographic expert on a holiday trek through the Himalayas, tapped a fiber trunk line landing in a remote section of Ecuadorian jungle, ferried cyphers from Singapore to Colombo, supplied heroic quantities of MDMA to a pettable posse of semiconductor engineers taking a pleasure cruise across the Adriatic, turned a Chinese agent posing as a UC Berkeley computer science PhD candidate, fled a counterintelligence squad through the colonial back-alleys of Montevideo, and laid honeytraps for state officials in Bangkok's best reputed house of ill repute.

If I wasn't traveling under pseudonyms, I would have accumulated enough frequent flyer miles to earn not only guaranteed first class seating, but complimentary shoulder massages for life. As it was, shuffling passports and time zones so often made it hard to keep my head and stories straight. Bit by bit, I slipped into the characteristic fugue state of the intelligence officer where your identity shifts and fades until you are nothing more than a texture sketched into the forgotten corners of other people's worlds.

Of course, there was one thing guaranteed to rip me from my fugue: Caroline. Employing the intermittent re-inforcement beloved by pet trainers and social media algorithms, she would appear at the most unlikely times to flip a victory into a defeat, a defeat into a victory, or me into a fit of totally unprofessional desire. When my intuition told me she'd materialize, she wouldn't. She only arrived when I least expected, despite my attempts to second and third guess my intuition. We never had time for more than a whisper or a tryst. The more we saw each other, the less I understood. We were an interference pattern, vanishing as soon as we offset the actions of the other, infinitely maddening and intoxicating.

Caroline was a dangerous enigma, but she was also becoming a strangely familiar enigma. She had a kidney bean shaped birthmark just below her left shoulder blade. She was unusually attentive and respectful to service staff. There was her incurable addiction to mystery novels and her preternatural ability to profoundly shift her emotional affect without changing her facial expression. She would interrupt my jokes with punchlines that were often better than what I had in mind. Our silences shed their awkwardness. Wherever we found ourselves, she always knew where to find decent coffee, even though she preferred tea. In the briefest of stolen moments under the least comfortable circumstances imaginable, we were somehow growing comfortable with each other. Then we'd vanish back into our own lives until the next surreal interlude.

Every time I cycled back through Mindanao, something was different. The aircraft carrier's fleet multiplied as if they were a school of nymphomaniacal guppies. Both Washington and Beijing carried out progressively more aggressive "training exercises" in the South China Sea. Diplomatic talks deteriorated into performative rhetoric. Tariffs leapt and then leapt again in retaliation. Visa requirements stiffened. Headlines went from cautious to strident. Stress levels rose in the other Residents, who were uniformly the sort of people in whom stress engenders calm, so the more pressure we found ourselves under, the smoother our little ship sailed, trawling for secrets, casting for leverage, steering for that distant shore called Power.

And if you were to climb the rigging and peer through your spyglass, you might catch a glimpse of something on the horizon, something that might just be your long-sought destination.

Land ho, sailor. Land ho.

40

Please forgive the aside, but I want to take a moment to assure you that this isn't one of those stories where it turns out that two hopelessly entangled characters are in fact—drumroll—*the same person*!

Cue credits and, the following spring, Oscars.

Yes, Caroline mysteriously invaded my life at opportune moments when nobody else of consequence was present, but that's because she's a sneaky motherfucker of the highest order.

Yes, I awkwardly avoided telling Leia and everyone else of consequence about her, trapping me in a prison of my own making, but that's because, as you've surely noticed, I have self-destructive tendencies and, of course, you're experiencing this story with the benefit of hindsight, whereas I had to live it blind, so fuck off.

Caroline is not a figment of my subconscious or an avatar of multiple personality disorder or an imaginary friend or a neat bow at the end of a screenplay. Caroline is a living, breathing, thinking, shitting, fucking, flesh-and-blood member of the big happy family we call Homo sapiens sapiens, and she's holding a very real gun to my admittedly sweaty forehead and asking questions so pointed they could pierce a narcissist's ego.

Yes, I am still locked in a hotel room with an armed maniac. Sheer linen curtains billow in gusts that cut the postcoital funk with ocean tang. In the distance, I can hear a poorly maintained motorcycle struggling to ascend the hill rising from the harbor. The briefcase lies patient and unobserved under the bed. Time isn't running out, but it is running down.

When you respond to a question with a story, it draws people in. Settling for a straightforward answer becomes impossible. They want to know what happens next. Once you toss the balls into the air, they need you, the juggler, to catch them. Even if they're holding a deadly weapon, their deep-seated desire for resolution precludes interruption. Just like my abuela did for me and my cousins on so many occasions, I'm wrapping my interrogator and myself in narrative, weaving a tale immersive enough that our imaginations displace our senses. I'm no Shakespeare. I'm not even a master storyteller like my abuela. But I don't need much. Just a split second of blunted attention.

Caroline's eyes are intent, but her mind is occupied. She's syncing to the story's rhythm. More often than not, her questions, however pointed, follow the anecdotes. The pressure of the barrel against my forehead has appreciably lessened. It's almost the right moment to make my move.

Almost.

"What about Samsung?" she asks, and something shifts in her, and for a fleeting moment I see the girl looking out through the woman's eyes. "How could you have done something like that?"

"I didn't know," I say.

There are moments in life when, if given the choice, you would willingly disintegrate into nothing, your story fading from history, your constituent atoms sloughing away, your being succumbing wholly and permanently to entropy.

"Come on," she says.

"I didn't know," I repeat, shrugging, wishing I'd known, wishing I'd objected, wishing I hadn't just shrugged, not wanting to be the person she knew me to be.

"Really," I say.

She appraises my sad smile.

"Then you didn't *want* to know," she says.

I can't argue with that.

41

Ready for a fun fact about sailboats sure to earn you admiration at your next cocktail party? If it wants to be, a small sailboat on the high seas is effectively invisible to other vessels. There's no chugging engine. Quiet as a vegan at a *churrascaria*, it skims along the surface powered by nothing more than Aeolus's throaty puffs.

If you're the captain of a nuclear submarine, this presents a problem. See, your job is to be a ghost. Because any radio ping could give away your position to a foreign power, when you're cruising the darkness beneath the waves, your mom doesn't know where you are. The Pentagon doesn't know where you are. *Nobody* knows where you are. Such a purveyor of apocalypse must be able to strike from anywhere and nowhere.

Every once in a long while, you ascend to the surface. Naturally, you do this as far as possible from any potential observers. Almost every time, the exercise goes smoothly and after sucking in a few precious breaths of fresh air, you return to Poseidon's lair. But if the stars align in just the wrong way, and they have only done so once or twice in all of naval history, your sleek machine rises from the depths and hits the hull of a small sailboat that you had no way of knowing was there.

Crunch goes the hull.

Whoosh goes the water.

Down goes the sailboat.

Now comes the nasty part: the secrecy of your geographical position is a matter of national security. You can't offer aid. You can't radio anyone who might be able to offer aid. So, from the safety of your unblemished multibillion dollar engine of mass destruction, you have no choice but to watch the innocent sailors drown in desperate silence. You stand ready to kill millions, you've trained for it your whole life, but you were never prepared for such intimate, senseless manslaughter.

You were a captain, once.

Now, you're a sea monster.

42

I wasn't the captain, but I did catch a ride on a nuclear sub. It was the only way to clandestinely traverse a South China Sea crowded with naval vessels running exercises and launching drones and inventing new ways of intimidating each other without actually killing anyone, a dynamic familiar to dueling middle school bullies the world over.

Ships are often described as worlds unto themselves, but, sealed off as they are, submarines embody this dream more fully than any other vessel—I mean, shit, even spacecraft have portholes through which to gaze at distant nebulae. The minute you dip beneath the waves, the rest of Planet Earth recedes, as if nothing exists beyond your steel cigar and history itself is merely whispered lore.

I was useless to the crew and cut off from everyone

else, so I caught up on badly needed sleep and read Alexis Valentine's controversial new translation of the *Aeneid*. It was from this brief respite that the XO roused me, bleary-eyed and still thinking in dactylic hexameter, to attend my rendezvous.

Thankfully, when we reached the surface, we did not breach the sailboat's hull. They were bobbing safely on rolling groundswell a few hundred meters away. I hauled myself through the hatch, pulled my Pelican cases up behind me, startled at the clarity of the Milky Way smeared across the night sky like excess semen from the Big Bang, found my footing on the slippery deck, and peered out into darkness.

They flashed the signal.

I flashed the countersign.

Ten minutes later, a dinghy materialized, a solitary woman pulling the oars. Despite my brain's plea for calm, my body reacted like I'd just snorted three lines of questionable coke.

But it wasn't Caroline.

It was Ae-cha, as planned.

My heart rate decelerated.

I handed over the Pelican cases.

She rowed away into darkness.

Nothing to see here. Just ghosts passing in the night.

Mission accomplished.

Sometimes, things just work out the way they should. With no ambushes, no hiccups, no last-minute emergencies, I thought this was one of those times.

This was not one of those times.

43

The sub ferried me back to Mindanao.

In retrospect, that uneventful passage was the last time I could meet my own eyes in a mirror. I knew who I was. I knew something of the world. But everything I knew was dwarfed by what I didn't.

I didn't know that even as we navigated the blue-black depths, Ae-cha and her team were using the chemical precursors I'd delivered to cook up explosives, explosives they used to bomb semiconductor fabs in Hwaseong, Giheung, and Pyeongtaek simultaneously, killing hundreds of innocent people and taking out all of Samsung's cutting-edge chip manufacturing.

The mission's fiery finale had been need-to-know, and I

hadn't needed to know, so I hadn't known.

I hadn't wanted to know.

With the possible exception of questionable coke, igno-rance is the most dangerous form of bliss.

44

You must be profoundly impressed by my espionage bona fides, and I don't blame you. I'm me, after all. If you need to recruit an informant of the highest caliber, smuggle a cryptographic key out of a war zone, or sniff out a mole, I'm your guy. Best of the best. Top shelf. But I do have one professional weakness, and it's a big one, the kind of thing that can sabotage a career: I'm not a sociopath.

(Even if you are also not a sociopath, I really can't recommend introducing yourself as "not a sociopath." It's the kind of statement that causes people to unkindly assume its opposite.)

If you're a teacher, nurse, journalist, public servant, developer, scientist, cook, or carpenter, this would be a huge liability, but in my line of work, genuinely not caring about anyone but yourself is a freakin' superpower. Enjoy meeting interesting people and lying to them? Relish collecting the latest hot goss and leveraging it to make people do things they'd rather not? Love pulling strings and watching others suffer the consequences? Then I highly recommend either espionage or finance, which have more in common than you think.

Look, I'm no saint. I don't even claim to be a "good person." (In my experience, people who go out of their way to lay claim to their essential goodness often aren't—a dynamic substantially parallel to claiming that you're "not a sociopath.") Lorenzo's death provoked an existential crisis, but it didn't ruin my sense of humor. Squeezing Barend didn't jiggle my moral compass. I've killed people before. Fewer than you'd think, but more than zero. And I've knowingly done things that led to the deaths of many more people. Any spy who denies they have blood on their hands is either lying to you or themselves, and probably both.

But Samsung was different.

Barend and Lorenzo and Phillip and those other poor fucks I've screwed in one way or another all had something in common: they were bastards. Just as there's honor among thieves, there's a shared feeling among bastards that anything's fair when you're dealing with a fellow bastard. Punch me in the face for no reason? Funnel my retirement savings into a pyramid scheme? Threaten to dox my nephew? Ohhh, you're a bastard, too. No worries, mate. I totally get it. Good on you. And I know you won't hold it against me when I come back to bite you in the ass. Because I will. I will bite you in the ass. I will draw blood. I'll make you wish you had hemorrhoids. It's not personal. We're just both total bastards.

The Samsung people weren't bastards. They were engineers, analysts, janitors, designers, interns, technicians, and executives. They were colleagues, parents, friends, and mentors. They even had a softball team. I looked it up. The uniforms were extremely tacky. The smiles may or may not have been forced. But at least some of them must have been having fun at least some of the time. Probably. I mean, they were people. They weren't perfect. They had their flaws and foibles. Some of them might even have been the type who lay not so credible claim to being "good people." You know what they *weren't*? They weren't bastards.

But I gave Ae-cha and her crew what they needed to snuff out all those lives. Boom. Boom. Boom. Simple as that. Goodbye, fabs. Goodbye, everyone who happened to be in or near said fabs. Goodbye, softball team. Goodbye, lots of people who weren't bastards, like not even close.

I was the submarine captain who sank the sailboat.

I wish I didn't care. I wish my conscience was a shake-to-erase board. That would make me the kind of spy who could make history. And even if the blessing of sociopathy was to lie forever beyond my reach, I wish I could have blamed my aiding and abetting on naïveté. But, as

Caroline said, *come on*. I might not have known the plan, but I knew what we were capable of. And the thing about capabilities is that once you have them, you use them.

45

As soon as the attack hit the news, I knew I was complicit. I was recuperating in my subterranean lair, holing up in the pod before the new mission briefing scheduled for the following morning. One minute I was absentmindedly trolling the internet for Caroline, and the next thing I knew, Samsung rocketed to the top of trending topics across every major platform.

My stomach twisted. Only five days had passed since my rendezvous with Ae-cha. I didn't want to follow the links, I would have done anything not to click, not to go down a path that I already knew deep down would only lead to darkness. But the more you try to ignore darkness, the more its menacing thunderheads build and roil along the horizon of your psyche. All too soon you find yourself in the shrinking eye of a gathering storm.

So I clicked. And clicked. And clicked and clicked and clicked and clicked. Grisly photos, horrifying accounts, and hot take after hot take papered over virtual Joshua Tree. The internet was ablaze, and in my gut I knew I had provided the match. The three simultaneous attacks had been carefully orchestrated and perfectly executed. This wasn't the work of disenfranchised teenagers raging against the machine. This required choreography, skill, resources, and coordination. This required expertise—expertise you hired people like Ae-cha for.

I swiped away everything and sat there hyperventilating. The desert stretched out around me, sunset painting the dome of the sky a vivid pink. But the desert, and the sunset, was a lie. I was buried under rock and soil and jungle. I was living in a tomb. This was a place of death, and I was its avatar, the hand with which it reached out into the world to tease and snatch and strangle. This was precisely the kind of atrocity my abuela had sought to escape by fleeing Cuba.

So, before I found a way to stop myself, I called Leia.

The Burghers sacrificed themselves for Calais, and I've always been willing to sacrifice myself on the altar of America, but I'm not willing to be tricked into sacrificing three factories full of innocent Korean citizens on that same altar. When the high priestess presses you into that kind of service, you start questioning your religion.

46

"Why?" I was a volcano, fear and anger seething within me, threatening to erupt.

Leia, matcha-guzzling black hole of ambition that she is, stared down at me quizzically from the rock she was perched on. "Unless you've decided to wax philosophical," she said, "I'm afraid you're going to have to be more specific."

I stifled my inner turmoil and said very carefully, "Why did I just blow up those factories?" Images of carnage and grief-stricken loved ones had burned themselves into my mind's eye.

"Ahh," she said. "I know you love to take credit, but you hardly deserve it all in this particular case. The operation was very much a team effort. I'm not saying you didn't play your part, but let's not pretend you're always the star of the show."

This took me aback. I had been expecting her to deny it. I'd thought I'd need to drag a confession out of her. But she acknowledged the attack as if it were business as usual, as if my visit to the Sea of Japan was just another job, and I was just another courier.

"Was there something else?" she asked, raising her eyebrows.

"You didn't think that maybe I'd want to know I was arming a terrorist?" I demanded. "Like 'BTW, this evening you'll help murder hundreds of innocent people.'"

Leia didn't flinch, but her face went perfectly still, which was much scarier. "Terrorism is theater," she said. "A party trick that uses violence to attract attention. I do not sanction terrorism. I would never waste our time on such trivialities."

"Then what the fuck just happened in Korea?"

Leia looked at me for a long moment and something shifted in her, a subtle change in her bearing, in the way she appraised me.

"Phase Two," she said at last.

I did not want to know what Phase Two was.

"And what, pray tell, is Phase Two?" I asked.

"Before today, there were two sources of cutting-edge chips on Earth," she said, shrugging. "I needed there to be one."

Blood pounded in my ears. She was playing with me, revealing just enough to require further revelation, stringing me along. I was a cat, and she had a laser pointer. If there's one thing I hate more than anything, it's feeling like a pawn in a game I don't understand.

"You're creating a bottleneck at TSMC," I said, reaching past horror into the cold logic of those who weaponize it. "Trying to incite open war over Taiwan."

It made an insane kind of sense. Leia had pinned her professional reputation on Mindanao, and the more the relationship between DC and Beijing deteriorated, the more important our little operation became. Concentrating global chip fabrication at TSMC—Taiwan Semiconductor Manufacturing Company—raised the stakes of a Chinese invasion.

"Oh, my sights are set far higher than that," she said. "I plan to win before a shot is fired. And not just this war, but the next one."

"How?"

"By hijacking every chip TSMC prints," she said.

I inhaled sharply.

Pieces snapped into place.

"Phillip," I said. "Barend…"

"Yes," she said. "Phase One."

"Fuck," I said.

"Yes," she said.

The puzzle came into view.

"*Fuck*," I said.

47

"Now you see why Samsung was a necessary tragedy," said Leia. "Yes, 997 innocent people died. But their sacrifice will save millions by averting a world war over Taiwan."

"South Korea is an American *ally*," I said.

"That's why it had to be them," she said. "Everyone will assume the aggressor was North Korea, and the world won't find Beijing's denials plausible."

"And that's why it had to be us," I said in a small voice.

She nodded. "The Mindanao program exists to do the hard but essential things that others won't," she said.

"Everyone needs someone to blame," I said, imagining Washington politicos game-theorizing their way through every path in the dark forest until, regardless of how many companions were lost along the way, they made it out the other side.

"No," she said. She cocked her head. "Or, at least, that's not the most important reason."

I swallowed, processing. "Politicians can't leak what they don't know," I said in a cadence halfway between question and statement. "If they have to lie to cover this up, they won't believe their own promises."

"What our nation stands for is too important to ring hollow," she said, with a slow nod of approval.

"So nobody else is even aware of what we're doing here," I said. "We're straight-up lying to them about it."

"What we are doing here," she said flatly, "gives them the capacity to make those promises come true."

"'The greater good' is a popular excuse for doing terrible things," I said.

"It's popular for a reason," she said. "And there's no excusing Samsung, just as there was no avoiding it."

"Easy for you to say," I said bitterly.

"Nothing about this is easy," she snapped. "Time to grow up and face it."

Stars winked on as dusk faded into desert night.

I have many faults, but I'm not often accused of naïveté. I pictured the softball team in their tacky jerseys. I knew the American government had done some awful things to get what it wanted, but I'd never played a direct role in something so unconscionable.

"What if I don't want to turn the world into your puppet

show?" I said.

I've skinny-dipped in a Norwegian fjord and trudged through a Himalayan blizzard, but I've never experienced anything as cold as that smile.

"What you want has nothing to do with it," she said.

48

"**We've known each other** a long time," I said, sinking into myself.

"We have," said Leia.

Galaxies wheeled above us in the desert night. I imagined the points of light winking out one by one, each corresponding to a life I'd taken at Hwaseong, Giheung, or Pyeongtaek.

"We've seen players come and go," I said, sinking down, down, down.

"We have," she said.

My pod smelled like sweat. And that fucking lavender. My abuela had always muddled lavender and mint into our lemonade. I thought all lemonade was made that way, and I still remember my disappointment when I first tasted a lemonade she hadn't prepared. Corpses don't turn over in their graves, dead is dead, but if she were alive today, I wouldn't be able to meet her penetrating gaze.

"Everyone has a breaking point," I said, sinking deeper still.

"They do," she said.

My own gaze drifted across starlit Joshua Trees, but I knew that behind this digital apparition lay stone and soil. We were buried here, dwelling in caves like trolls in some fantasy epic, casting dark spells to bring the world under our master's command.

"This is mine," I said, touching bottom.

"No, it isn't," she said.

A flash of anger burned down into an ember of resolve.

"I'm not going to do this for you," I said.

"Yes, you are," she said.

"I'm tired, Leia," I said.

"Entirely understandable," she said.

"Why didn't you tell me what we were about to do?" I said. "And don't give me any need-to-know bullshit."

"What did I tell you when you arrived on Mindanao?" said Leia.

"You told me a lot of things," I said, remembering the submersible surfacing in the submarine bay, the disorientation when Leia was there waiting for me, finally realizing she was an avatar.

"Yes, but there was a singular conclusion," she said. "'Don't fuck this up.'"

"OK," I said wearily. "Whatever you say, Leia."

"Except that you already had," she said.

"Excuse me?" I said.

"Lorenzo was murdered to protect an asset at TSMC," she said.

At the mention of his name, a chill passed through me, as if his ghost had been summoned, insistently tugging me back to my desperate search, the tripping teenagers, my abuela's tombstone.

"We've been wanting to recruit someone inside TSMC for years," Leia continued. "There are rumors that a foreign intelligence service has a highly placed asset who'd be perfect for this assignment. Lorenzo claimed to have identified the asset, a semiconductor manufacturing engineer. He came to Miami to sell you the name, but your barista killed him."

My stomach clenched, and it took everything I had to keep the shock from reaching my face. "My barista?" I managed to say, my voice seeming to come from far, far away.

"The one you slept with," said Leia. "The one you let borrow Phillip's designs. The one you've been seeing on and off during your entire tenure as a Resident. Adrian, I'm fine with you being a slut, what I'm not fine with is you failing to tell me about it."

I opened my mouth to object, to deny everything.

Memories welled up like blood in an open wound. That first moment of eye contact with Caroline over the gleaming espresso machine. The smell in the van as I drove

Lorenzo's corpse to the crematorium. The quiet pride I'd felt on receiving my commission as an intelligence officer.

No words escaped me.

What can you possibly say when someone accuses you of treason with perfect equanimity?

"Your barista—her real name is Roos de Vries, by the way—is a Dutch spy," said Leia. "The Netherlands is an ally. We have intel sharing agreements in place with their security services, so I could afford to indulge your dalliance as long as you didn't pass along anything we didn't want Holland in the loop on. But I certainly couldn't be honest with you about Samsung, or what we've been building toward this whole time."

Leia was drawing a fault line through my life, and my world was collapsing around it.

"I like you, Adrian," she said. "Sometimes, anyway. But I can't afford to indulge you any longer."

I didn't know which would be worse: a closed trial in a federal court or a shallow grave in a black site. Either way, it would be a strange kind of relief to let my hoard of secrets go, cutting the web of strings I'd woven so assiduously.

"Then it's all over," I said, wondering if Samantha would be the one to execute me, and whether she'd do me the mercy of making it quick.

"Not even close," said Leia.

"But–"

"Don't be an idiot," she said. "All this"—she circled a finger to draw a noose around our conversation—"I don't hold it against you. I hold it *over* you."

I was Damocles glancing up at the sword hanging from a coarse strand of horsehair.

"Back in Langley, I asked if I could trust you," said Leia. "You were honest with me. You said no. So I'll be honest with you. From now on, you're going to do exactly what I want, or I burn you. It's that simple."

"Why would you send someone like me on a mission like this?" I said, imagining the honed tip of the blade dangling a few inches above my raised eyes.

Leia sighed. "Making trust a prerequisite would severely limit my ability to delegate," she said. "But there is a very specific reason why you can't bow out of this particular job. Roos de Vries is the case officer running the TSMC asset so jealously, and I need you to convince her to share."

49

I lay on my bunk staring up at the dome of stars long after Leia vanished into the digital aether.

John Dee was a Welsh mathematician who consulted for Queen Elizabeth I. Like many natural philosophers of that era, his interests ranged far beyond math into geography, astronomy, astrology, and the occult. No wonder then, that my favorite of his ideas blends science and magic. He proposed launching a mirror out into space faster than the speed of light so that you could watch all of history unfold across it in reverse.

If we allow the mirror's impossible speed to breach the laws of physics, why not allow me to breach them again by reaching into the past and unmaking all my bad decisions? I could have reported my affair with Caroline at any time. I could have questioned a random barista's interest in casual sex. I could have chosen to build things, to teach kids, to make art instead of choosing a life of secrets and lies and betrayals. I could have told my abuela what she meant to me, why I looked up to her, how much I loved her lemonade. My family sacrificed everything to give me and my cousins opportunity, and this is what I made of it.

This.

This game.

This sad, ancient game where everyone cheats and nobody wins.

The dark tide within me was surging, and the most horrifying thing about it was that I knew it would eventually recede. I could ask no questions. I could merely proceed. I knew that if I tried, if I gave it time, I could find a way to justify this to myself. Anyone could. Judge me all you want, but if you're honest with yourself, you could, too. Humans are supremely adaptable. I could adapt to this. I could pretend it was OK until I was OK, until I had redefined "OK" to include this. I could soak up the darkness, consume it before it consumed me, absorb it into my being. I could learn to live with this.

But I didn't *want* to.

If anyone can learn to live with anything, then your life is defined by what you choose to live with.

I squeezed my eyes shut and screamed until my throat was raw.

No one came to check on me. The pods were sound-proof. Except they weren't pods, after all.

They were cells.

50

You know that feeling when you're listening to a song and, even though you've never heard it before, you know *exactly* what the next note is going to be? The artist might appear to be playing their instrument, but they're really playing your heartstrings—building tension, offering release, stitching motifs together to set and subvert your expectations until you feel the music so deeply that you know its future.

Musicians don't have a monopoly on this dark magic. The right movie, book, painting, or podcast can be just as immersive and compelling. The invisible force at work inside all of them is called story: that mirror image of the spectacular neurochemical firework display of a living mind.

And *this* story—the one I'm telling Caroline, the one I'm telling you—is a special kind of story.

This story is a trap, and just as Leia's had snapped shut around me, mine would snap shut around Caroline.

51

The curtains ripple like a courtesan's robe, revealing provocative glimpses of wine-dark sea. A bead of sweat slides down my left shoulder blade and my toes wiggle in the high pile of the Turkish rug. The framed charcoal sketch hanging above the headboard aspires to contain the entire room within its abstract spirals.

Now.

The dark eye of the barrel stares me down and, beyond that semiautomatic Cyclops, afternoon light slants in to drench Caroline in gold. I wait until my story reaches its zenith, letting the feeling of imminent betrayal build, reversal after reversal, sailboats and submarines and secret packages swimming before our minds' eyes, and then–

Is.

I move. I have rehearsed this a hundred times in my head as I answer question after question, narrative and visualization running in parallel. On Mindanao, Samantha drilled this disarm into me until the movements graduated from conscious act to habit.

The.

To achieve speed, don't try to go faster. Watch any great athlete. Not just a good athlete. A *great* one. No matter how quickly they accelerate past the competition, they aren't in a rush. They aren't seeking speed. They are seeking *grace*, and speed is a side effect.

I seek grace.

Time.

Muzzle.

Wrist.

Rotate.

Strip.

Caroline pulls the trigger, but, as I mentioned at the beginning of this sordid tale, the safety's still on.

52

Aspiring coffee nerds love to geek out on gear. They experiment with different brew methods. They participate in ruthless online debates about the relative merits of espresso setups. They blind taste test different roasts of the same beans and spend thousands of dollars on hand-built grinders with oversized burrs. They are on a perpetual quest for the perfect cup, and every morning's ritual represents an opportunity to make good on that promise, to inch closer and closer to the dark, steamy utopia their hearts ache for.

True coffee nerds realize the quest is hopeless. They recognize that perfection is abstract, a conceptual ideal, while coffee is a hot fluid sloshing around your chipped mug. By abandoning the quest and thereby graduating from aspiring to true coffee nerds, they attain the grail they were seeking all along: a deep appreciation of every sip of coffee that blesses their lips, whether it's a macchiato prepared by an award-winning barista, or, gods forbid, Nespresso. Instead of using their finely tuned palettes to pinpoint subtle flaws, they zero in on the best attributes of even the humblest cup. You can identify true coffee nerds by the quiet smile that graces their faces after the first sip of the bitterest brew.

Once you see perfection for what it is, a mirage, you start to notice new possibilities in the real world it was obscuring. For example, coffee is mostly water. All the fancy gear on the planet won't make for a good cup if you start with mediocre water. And if you distill your water to take out the impurities, you'll end up with a flat cup because the flavor compounds in the grounds have nothing to latch onto as you brew it. The impurities in your water are precisely what makes the water great for making coffee. Of course there are companies that sell mineral packets you can add to distilled water engineered to squeeze the most flavor out of your grounds, but true coffee nerds know that you can simply add a pinch of salt to the brew and achieve the same result.

There's a deep pattern at work here. You'll only extract coffee's richest flavors if they have mineral impurities to bond with. Snowflakes form around tiny specks of dust churning in the atmosphere. A few words of affirmation from a seventh-grade teacher changes the life path of the student third from the left in the back row. There are moments that the world hinges on, singularities around which new ways of being crystalize, paths fanning out into a future you can't predict, only invent.

This was just such a moment.

53 ≡≡≡≡

≡≡≡≡ **Holy fuck: it worked.**

Despite my scheming, I never truly *believed* it would work. I knew it *could* work. I knew it was *possible*. But I'm so accustomed to things going wrong that things going right took me by surprise.

Caroline stumbles back and lands awkwardly on the edge of the bed. I surge forward, flicking off the safety and leveling the gun at her forehead.

FUCK YEAH! I want to scream. I'M A GODDAMN NINJA. I EAT RAZOR BLADES FOR BREAKFAST. I BATHE IN THE LUKEWARM BLOOD OF MY ENEMIES. I WIN BECAUSE WINNING IS ALL THERE IS AND ALL I HAVE EVER KNOWN. BOW BEFORE MY SUPREME BADASSERY.

But reveling in victory, no matter how sweet, is decidedly amateur, and Caroline and I are professionals. Professionals know that a turned table can be turned again. Professionals know that the way you treat anyone is the way you treat everyone. Professionals know that Caesar did a lot of conquering only to be murdered by a friend.

Caroline isn't the only one with questions. I know her better than I've ever known anyone, I know her better than I know myself, and yet I don't know her at all. She has invaded my life, to be sure. Starting with that little coffee shop in Miami, every cameo she's made has heralded bigger and gnarlier problems for me. But that's not the worst of it. The worst part is that she has quietly infiltrated my mind. She's the Joker in my deck. Whenever the dealer turns over a card, I wonder whether her winking face will be printed on it, whether it'll save or destroy my hand.

That means Caroline has stolen something more valuable than Lorenzo's intel or Phillip's chip designs. She has stolen my *attention*. Her innumerable ghosts are already haunting the internet. Now, they're haunting my thoughts. And this isn't a side effect. This isn't incidental or accidental. We've traveled light-years beyond coincidence. She's doing this on purpose. And I want to know why.

I cock my head to the side and allow myself a tight smile.

"Wanna dance?"

The look in her eyes sends me down memory's rabbit hole.

54

The morning after Leia took my future hostage, I joined the other Residents in the conference room. Our cadre had gelled over the past few months of nonstop operations, shared experience and a common resentment of our masters' perennial unreasonableness binding us together. (Effective bosses, like Leia, know this, so they make sure to act like assholes every so often so the team under their command can bitch about them and, in doing so, grow closer.) I no longer worried that the group was convening to kick me off the island—Leia's elegant manipulations made that kind of ambush unnecessary.

My boss leaned forward across the conference table that connected Virginia to the Philippines. Her star was rising at precisely the same rate as geopolitical tension around the Pacific Rim. As Washington and Beijing prepared for what felt like an inevitable war, Leia was displacing all the other would-be Beltway powerbrokers, including the other Residents' patrons. They hadn't even been invited to this meeting. I wasn't the only one she'd outplayed.

"Welcome to Phase Three," she said.

Leia was glowing. She clicked through slides like each was a divine gift. She zigzagged between ideas and their compounding implications. She answered questions with steely confidence. World order was a grand piano, and her fingers were dancing over the keys. A new century of American hegemony was within reach. I imagined her placing the President on hold. I imagined that her walking meetings must have become notably brisk.

Leia's glow was terrifying because it was the kind of aura emitted by radioactive materials. I had once assumed we were running parallel races. She, along the Beltway track. I, along the twisting cross-country course of field work. Seeing her pull out ahead of the pack made me realize how I detested the race in which I was supposedly competing. I wasn't an Olympian pursuing a gold medal, not anymore. I was a racehorse that would be put down as soon as I stopped winning. Instead of preparing for the final sprint, I wanted to wander off on a side path in search of greener pastures. It was a feeling all too common in Leia's native California: ground shifting under your feet.

"Give it to him," said Leia.

I snapped back to reality just in time to see Bisrat heft a briefcase onto the table. There's a special beauty that objects only acquire through regular, loving use—a patina of imperfections that describe a long arc of experience, maintenance, repair, intimacy, and appreciation. With its supple leather and handle worn shiny by countless palms, this briefcase gave off serious loving-use vibes. It was a thing comfortable with itself, at peace with its place in the universe, a briefcase that wasn't pretending to be anything other than a briefcase.

This, of course, was a lie—anything that goes out of its way to look that innocuous is anything but.

Bisrat opened the briefcase and peeled away a strip of twill lining to reveal a false bottom, which, when she caressed it with her fingertips, cracked open with a faint hiss.

Inside lay a living morning glory, beautiful and menacing, green tendrils spiraling across black silk, roots tangling in a micro-hydroponic system, opulent flowers illuminated by recessed grow lights, intricate pink, purple, and white patterns inscribed on their petals like floral runes.

55

Don't tell my bosses or my family, but Taiwan is my favorite country in the world. If you mention Taiwan, most Americans think you're talking about Thailand. Despite its tenuous and pivotal geopolitical position, Taiwan isn't on the general public's radar. I've been to a lot of places. I can recite every international airline's preflight safety video word for word (a condition I wouldn't wish on anyone, even you). So believe me when I tell you that Taiwan is the single most underrated destination on this dinky little planet zipping through the Orion Arm of the Milky Way.

Taiwan may not have the pyramids, or the Louvre, or the Taj Mahal, or other photogenic tourist traps. But you've seen that stuff already. The internet is overflowing with better pictures of those things than you'll ever take. So why spend the oh-so-precious two weeks of freedom the corporate overlords deign to extend your way following the same rut every aspiring travel influencer has already worn smooth?

No. Don't even try to object. I refuse to believe that anyone with such generic taste would make it this far in this particular narrative. Almost everyone has never heard of this story. Of the few that have, yet fewer chose to embark on the journey. And then there are those odd ducks who kept going and then kept going some more until they arrived at this particular sentence. Yes, this sentence you're reading right now. We're here, now, together. And that means that you're my kind of weirdo, and my kind of weirdo doesn't settle for tour group vacations. If you've been on tour group vacations, then I'm telling you right now that underneath the conformist exterior you've cultivated for yourself is a beautiful weirdo waiting patiently to break out and expand your horizons. Lend that weirdo a hand. They will blow your mind. It'll be scary, but you'll love it.

And because we've established that you're my kind of weirdo, whether or not you've admitted it to yourself yet, I can tell you with complete confidence that you'll love Taiwan. Secret dumpling houses and coffee shops and speakeasies and bookstores hidden in urban mazes that make every stroll a treasure hunt. Mist rising from neon green tea plantations. Impeccably efficient public transportation. Killer sense of style. Waves the size of houses smashing against cliffs that tower into azure sky. Strong hopepunk vibes. The best fried chicken you've ever tasted. A vibrant democracy where proactive citizenship is a privilege, not a chore. Mountain ridges folded one behind the other as if some curious deity had reached down and crumpled rock like a child does paper.

Glad to hear you booked a ticket. You won't regret it.

But sadly, I wasn't walking Taipei's streets—briefcase in one hand, umbrella in the other, fat raindrops splintering city lights into a glittering collage—in order to enjoy this small nation's distinctive pleasures.

I was on a mission I'd refused, and somewhere deep down I knew it would be my last.

56

This was to be a joint operation with AIVD, the Dutch intelligence service. For reasons we've already gone over, the House of Orange has a keen and specific interest in the chip supply chain, so it didn't surprise me that one of their officers had that which we desire: an agent inside TSMC. What surprised me was that the officer in question was the woman I'd been chasing through shadows for so long.

I've heard that writers advise each other not to hoard material—they say that leading with your best ideas leads to even better ones. Spies know better. We respect the material. We *value* it. We know that hoarding material is often the best move, and the only better move is using it to gain access to yet more material. We are the robber barons of information, and when we find ourselves in possession of a monopoly, we are not afraid to squeeze.

However extravagant, I knew we would pay whatever price Caroline demanded—I could already imagine Leia's pained smile as she balanced secret against secret on the high-precision scale of her rapidly cooling heart—because even more important than AIVD's monopoly on their perfectly placed agent was TSMC's monopoly on cutting-edge chip manufacturing, a monopoly secured by the Samsung bombing.

Despite its name, Silicon Valley no longer makes semiconductors. Oh, sure, engineers in Cupertino and Mountain View and San Francisco *design* computer chips, but they outsourced the *manufacturing* of those chips decades ago. Many Americans assume that only low-skill work gets outsourced, that the country doing the outsourcing retains the capability of doing the work itself and, if necessary, could easily do it again in future. This assumption may be true in some industries, but it is dead false when it comes to semiconductors.

Just as ASML has a stranglehold on the lithography machines required to make chips, TSMC is one of only two producers capable of manufacturing advanced chips at scale. The other producer was Samsung. TSMC's fabs each cost tens of billions of dollars to build, their engineers have expert knowledge that no other team on Earth can match, and their chips power everything from the phone in your pocket to the servers enabling your next internet search to the fridge holding your leftovers to the plane that ferried you to that vacation you still need a vacation from. If you need computer chips, TSMC is the place to get them, and these days, literally everyone needs computer chips.

How awkward, then, that TSMC is where it is: Taiwan—an independent country that China claims as its territory. This geopolitical faux pax is no accident. Taiwan intentionally set out to make itself indispensable to the global economy so that the United States and its allies couldn't afford to cede the island to Beijing. So when Texas Instruments and other American chipmakers started scouting for places to offshore manufacturing, Taipei invested heavily. And then they doubled down. And then doubled down again. Over the past fifty years, they've become by far the best in the world at making chips, and it would take any other country, including China and the United States, at least a decade to catch up no matter how much they're willing to spend. So the reality is that the weapons Beijing is pointing at Taiwan have TSMC chips in them, and the satellites the Pentagon has tracking those weapons have TSMC chips in them, and the laptop you spend too much of your time staring at has a TSMC chip in it.

Sneaky, right? Mad respect.

The only problem is that Taiwan succeeded in making itself indispensable only to discover that those who seek dominance covet the indispensable as a means of control, which explains the Chinese and American aircraft carriers facing off against each other a few miles away in the Taiwan Strait, and the flocks of drones swarming above them, and me, throwing a glance back over my shoulder into the dark, wet night before approaching the unmarked door for the AIVD rendezvous.

57

I put my hand on the doorknob.

Ever since Leia's revelation, I'd been trying not to think about Caroline. I didn't want her ghosts haunting my psyche. I was tired of her upending the only life I'd ever known. But it was more than resenting the shitstorm she'd brought down on my head. The reason I'd been trying not to think about Caroline was that I didn't want the mystery of her packed neatly into a box. I felt like a kid discovering that Santa isn't real—the melancholy of eroding myth.

It made sense that she was a Dutch intelligence officer, and that this whole business was spy vs spy. It explained the nation-state level resources required to spawn her endless stream of digital doubles, and how she always seemed to know more than she should, at least some of the motivations behind our intersecting missions, and even why our liaisons had appeared to stay under the radar for so long. There were still enough holes in the story to give an editor an aneurism, but this wasn't journalism, this was espionage, and the stories spooks care about consist almost entirely of holes.

The fact that it made a pretzeled kind of sense was the problem. Can you ever truly understand another person? I couldn't tell you, but failing to understand Caroline had been bringing me to terms with failing to understand myself.

I turned the knob.

The door was unlocked.

58

I stepped into a children's picture book.

Every inch of the walls and ceiling were covered in whimsical illustrations. A mouse wearing a jester's hat rode on the back of an elephant. Foxes peeked out through thick ferns, their bushy tails bright red against deep green. Flying fish leapt from stylized waves, scales sparkling. An owl gazed down through thick spectacles from the crook of an ash. Monkeys juggled coconuts. Geese migrated across the baby blue sky in a ragged V. A bear scooped salmon from a river. Passionfruit vines twined along an outcrop of rock. Jaguar eyes glowed from the shadows.

It took me a moment to realize it wasn't just custom wallpaper. The walls themselves were layered: sections of wood cut and fitted to give depth to the illustrations. The trees popped out from the forest and the clouds popped out from the sky and the animals popped out from the backgrounds they were set against. The room was a kindergartener's menagerie in painstakingly crafted bas-relief.

There were no windows. A glowing sun set amongst the clouds provided the only illumination. Bach's Cello Suites emanated from unseen speakers, drowning out the pitter-patter of rain.

In the center of the room was a small wooden table with a *gongfu* tea set sculpted from red clay. And sitting at the table, looking up as the door snicked shut behind me, was Caroline.

59

"I was small for my age growing up," said Caroline. "When I was twelve years old, there were two girls in my class who hated each other. They were intent on sabotaging one another at all costs. Nothing burns hotter than adolescent hatred."

"And nobody is crueler than preteens," I said, remembering the bleak hellscape known as seventh grade.

She nodded. "They make Genghis Khan look like Santa Claus. Anyway, like any group of kids our age, we had all self-segregated into cliques aligned along a precise status hierarchy. Those two girls weren't the smartest or the most athletic or the most popular or the most beautiful, but they were totally obsessed with destroying each other, and because nobody else wanted anything as much as they did, eventually every clique fell into one camp or the other. There was no middle ground."

"Middle school isn't a kind enough world for a Switzerland?" I asked.

"Exactly," she said. "There was all the stuff you'd expect: whisper campaigns, stolen tampons, spiked Gatorade, drugs planted in lockers and then reported to teachers, older siblings recruited for intimidation, etc. etc. Like anything, it escalated. Then a nerdy kid from an unpopular clique managed to hack one of their phones, copied their text history, and, in a gambit that would guarantee a major status upgrade, published the texts to the open web, posted about it on Reddit, and sent the link to the entire school from an anonymous email address. At first, we all thought it was hilarious. But we quickly discovered texts in which our peers said brutal things about each of us, stuff we never would have said to each other's faces. It didn't take long for the news to spread to teachers and parents, all of whom had been likewise eviscerated in the exchanges. Then the press got hold of it and, the Netherlands being a small country, the story soon made national headlines. Two days later, the doxxed girl hung herself from the basketball hoop in the gymnasium. We all trooped in for morning exercise and saw her corpse dangling there." She paused. "I'll never forget that moment. It was so strange. So alien. It took time to register. And then someone screamed. The following week, her nemesis jumped in front of a train."

"Fuck," I said. "My childhood wasn't this"—I indicated the whimsical world of the tea room—"but it wasn't *that*. I'm sorry for you, and everyone involved."

And I was sorry, though I also knew that this revelation, which felt and even might *be* true, was being shared for a *reason*. It may sound counterintuitive, but I've come to appreciate weaponized vulnerability in this business because arming the weapon requires genuine disclosure.

Caroline adjusted a dial and a small bronze spout rose from the surface of the table, dispensing steaming water that she caught in the red clay teapot. She poured the hot water into the matching teacups, and then emptied everything onto the surface of the table, where the water drained through a wooden grid. She loaded tea leaves into the teapot, filled it with more hot water, drained it off after a few seconds to rinse them, and then filled it a third time to steep.

"Looking back, I can't ignore the fact that we all went along with it. Not all of us went as far as doxxing a class-mate, but we laughed at cruel jokes, egged on dumb kids doing bad things, helped pull pranks, did nothing to stop it. We aided and abetted. I remember it felt like being caught in a powerful current that carries you downstream until rapids appear out of nowhere and it's too late to swim to shore." She looked up at me, eyes bright, and I flashed back to the wink glimpsed from the Threshold cafeteria. "I never want to feel that way again."

Caroline poured the tea into the waiting cups and we drank. It was clean, delicate, and grassy, and, while it wasn't coffee, the warmth felt good after the downpour. I tried to center myself, to establish a baseline orientation in this strange room in this strange country with this strange antagonist, but despite, or perhaps because of, how Leia had reshuffled my life's deck, I felt detached, untethered.

"I was small for my age," said Caroline. "And I *acted* small by pretending nothing I could do would make a difference. I decided I would never make that mistake again. That's why I joined AIVD. That's why I'm here, now. The Netherlands is a small country, but we don't *act* small. The governments of the United States and China are preparing to destroy each other just like those two girls. It's time to swim to shore before we hit the rapids. We need to rewrite the script and we have an opening: Beijing is on the defensive because of the North Korean attack on Samsung. China has been preparing to invade Taiwan, but it isn't ready for a war on two fronts, especially if more countries unite against it. Moreover, losing Samsung makes the TSMC fabs all the more irreplaceable, and Chinese military planners must realize that making a move on Taiwan now would guarantee an even stronger international response. If Washington offers an off-ramp to de-escalation, Beijing will take it. If you want access to my agent at TSMC, I need you to build that off-ramp."

There it was: the reason.

60

Caroline's ask was ridiculous.

More than ridiculous: insane.

Demanding that I, a lowly intelligence officer, alter the geopolitical course of my patron nation state in exchange for access to a single asset? How the hell am I supposed to make that happen? I'm not God. I'm not even POTUS. I'm *me*.

It was like asking for your entire net worth, and that of your extended family, in exchange for a glass of tap water. Straight up silly. Laughable. Like, that's not how these things go. If the punishment should fit the crime, then the ask should fit the offer. Negotiations require proportionality. Otherwise, we're all just rubbing lamps and lobbing wishes at harried genies.

Why even bother negotiating when your interlocutor opens with this kind of move? Better to cut your losses and find another way.

But this mission was the culmination of everything we'd been working toward. By injecting our tweak into the systems controlling TSMC's manufacturing equipment, we could print our backdoor into silicon itself, giving the US government the means to hijack anything running a cutting-edge chip, which amounts to pretty much everything worth paying attention to.

Every new chip coming off the TSMC line would weave the world ever more tightly into Leia's net. It wasn't just watching your every move or stealing your sensitive data. Root access written to hardware meant that in addition to spying on you, we would be able to architect the virtual reality your devices compute within. We could adjust high finance as we pleased, directly controlling market cycles. We could manage the flow of information across the internet like a cop directing traffic. We could co-opt entire branches of scientific research and technological innovation. We could blow up enemy missiles stacked in silos, pwn drone fleets, and lobotomize AIs. There would be no logs. If anyone got suspicious, no matter how deep they dug, their systems would report *our* truth as *the* truth, because as far as the transistors were concerned, it would be. Not content with superpowerdom, we were determined to claim sovereignty over the fabric of reality itself, or at least the generous slice of reality computers could access. You used to be able to conquer the world with an army. Now you need an army and a bag of tricks. And for better and for worse, I was the guy holding the bag.

This is all to say that United States of Motherfucking America had a lot riding on what went down in this whimsical little Taiwanese tearoom. It was a gambit to end all gambits, but without Caroline's asset, I'd leave the table with a stack of chips and nowhere to cash them. Oh, and then Leia would flay me as expertly as any medieval torturer. If you're dying of thirst, you'll gladly exchange your entire net worth, and that of your extended family, for a glass of tap water.

Caroline didn't know *why* we wanted her asset so badly, but the sheer outrageousness of her request made it clear that she was sufficiently skilled at reading between the lines to realize that we, in fact, did *want* her asset that badly. She was asking the impossible because she was guessing at the impossibly high stakes.

What Caroline didn't realize was that the de-escalation she so desired wasn't just already part of Leia's plan, but crucial to its success. Bisrat and her team were already busy planting evidence to confirm the widely held assumption that North Korean terrorists were behind the Samsung attack. Samantha's military intelligence sources were corroborating Caroline's conclusion that this changed the calculus of Chinese military planners. And Jerry's pet diplomats were calling in favors and making veiled suggestions and doing everything they could to ensure that, given these unexpected bumps in the road, Beijing politicos would, in fact, decide to take an American-built off-ramp.

61

The Trojan Horse only worked because Troy opened its gates and accepted the gift. If, instead, Paris had sneered down at the Greeks from the ramparts, whether because he suspected an ulterior motive or simply didn't approve of the craftsmanship, the story would have ended very differently, and, after a few glasses of good wine, he'd still be kissing the face that launched a thousand ships.

Theft by theft, lie by lie, piece by piece, my fellow Residents and I had constructed a horse of our own, but for it to deliver the goods, we needed to convince the enemy to open their gates. Baking our master key into every chip TSMC fabricated would only grant us access to Chinese systems if China ran its systems on TSMC chips.

Ever since Washington blocked China from importing those chips, they'd been forced to rely on reserves, any new batches they were able to clandestinely obtain despite American restrictions, and inferior domestically produced substitutes.

And that brings us to the climax of Leia's plan. Ratchet up semiconductor trade restrictions and geopolitical pressure in the Taiwan Strait. Blame North Korea for the Samsung attack that simultaneously concentrates chip production at TSMC and puts China on its heels. Insert an exploit into TSMC chips. Offer to relax trade restrictions in exchange for de-escalation over Taiwan. Watch Beijing greedily install millions of cutting-edge chips into critical systems. Rub your hands in glee. Cackle. Sip a celebratory beverage. Congratulations, you are inside the Great Firewall. So, when Beijing inevitably decides to renege on de-escalation and finally make good on its ambitions to conquer Taiwan, you can literally turn off its military with the flip of a switch. And when everyone else sees what you've done and realizes the devices in their pockets are also in your pocket, there you have it: Pax Silicon, a new era of American hegemony.

Caroline wanted an off-ramp because the status quo benefited the Netherlands, and war would disrupt the status quo. Leia wanted an off-ramp because it led straight into a trap. That rendered my impossible negotiation easy. Caroline was asking us to do what we were already planning to do. The only hard part was convincing her that what she asked was insanely difficult but just barely possible to grant. So I ranted and raged and joked and threatened and quibbled and bitched and spilled my tea and made every kind of emotional appeal I could muster until I finally, desperately, surrendered to her demands, having reduced their scope to something she'd believe I could actually achieve.

I would build the off-ramp.

She would introduce me to her fabled TSMC asset.

Deal, done.

Well, almost.

"Oh, and there's one more thing," I said.

"Yes?"

"I can't," I said.

"You can't what?"

"I can't call you Roos," I said.

She shrugged, but I spotted the hastily suppressed split second of surprise at my knowledge of her true identity. "It's my name."

"Not to me, Caroline."

62

Like Silicon Valley, TSMC's fabled fabs are a Very Important Place that looks like a Not Very Important Place—basically a second-tier industrial park. It's strange how the world can turn on dimes this banal. If history had any sense of propriety, exciting things would happen in exciting settings, preferably scored by John Williams. Instead, superpowers grapple over beige carpeted complexes with generic water features and ten-mile-an-hour parking lot speed limits.

I was careful to level-set my appearance to match the blah-blah-blah office vibes. Meh gray suit. Meh leather shoes. ASML consulting badge. Fortunately, pretending to hail from the Netherlands provided the perfect excuse for a crucial eccentricity in my outfit: the morning glory boutonnière.

No, the flower didn't set off the metal detectors, and if the security guards had deigned to sniff it, the only thing they would have detected was a modest amount of pollen. It was all too easy to take the elevator to the appropriate floor, navigate the maze of bland conference rooms, and make my way to the office of Caroline's infamous agent, Liu Fu-hai.

I left my jacket hanging on his chair, and we walked down to the cafeteria to grab a coffee, where I walked Liu through a deck on my tablet that mapped out ASML's product roadmap: when TSMC could expect the next generation of EUV lithography to arrive, what the specs would be, how it would integrate into TSMC's workflow, and technical updates from the last roadmap review. (I'd never have been able to chat so fluently at this level of technical depth without Bisrat's patient coaching.) Then we refilled our coffees and traded gossip from our respective HQs, who was out on parental leave, who was on a performance improvement plan, who had a project fast-tracked by senior management, etc. Having dispensed with the formalities of my cover, we parted ways—Liu back to his office and me back to the parking lot.

Were you expecting a shootout? A boss battle? A car chase? Heavily armed security guards sprinting after me? At the very least an explosion? I regret to inform you that espionage done well is mostly boring. If your situation deserves to be scored by John Williams, something has gone very, very wrong.

But yes, you're right, oh attentive reader: I had conveniently forgotten to retrieve my jacket.

Driving back to the hotel, I imagined everything orbiting this particular moment in this particular place. Diplomats hashing out a new semiconductor trade agreement behind closed doors. Drones swarming back to the aircraft carriers that were beginning to exit the Strait. Headlines pivoting nimbly from warmongering to peacemongering. Markets soaring as the future, that mercurial asshole, appeared to be finding a new equilibrium.

My abuela used to host a big family dinner every Sunday. If you were a blood relative, you skipped it at your peril. Our family has no shortage of opinions, especially about the motherland, so we heard every possible hot take on every aspect of the Cuban Missile Crisis over and over and over again. My aunts and uncles milked the topic dry, so I don't have much to add, but what I can tell you is how odd it seems in retrospect for two geopolitical titans to have faced off over an island like Cuba, which, for all its many virtues, was essentially irrelevant to world affairs except for the fact that it was their focal point.

Taiwan was different. The fabs I'd just visited manufactured civilization's silicon minds. With stakes that high, it made perfect sense that Beijing and Washington were at odds over this oddball island. The Taiwanese Chip Crisis trumped the Cuban Missile Crisis, and while it would never stop my aunts and uncles from declaring strong opinions about this foreign affairs hiccup, they would never know the full story.

They would never know about Operation Glass Ceiling. They would never know that their nephew and his team had pilfered chip designs from every major firm and designed an exploit to take advantage of each of them. They would never know that a common morning glory had been genetically engineered to express the exploit in the patterns on its petals so that their nephew could smuggle it into the high-security TSMC facility. They would never know that Liu was at this very moment taking a picture of the boutonnière, decrypting the exploit from its brilliant white and purple stripes, inserting a subtle modification into the software governing the TSMC production process, and burning a backdoor into every chip the foundry churned out. They would never know about the scope of Leia's gambit, nor the war crimes their nephew had committed to seal the Pax Silicon.

And if they *did* know, if my abuela knew the decisions I'd made, the life I'd chosen... I should have been feeling glorious, or at least relieved. I had secured a coup for my nation. I had managed to outrun Leia's threats, at least for the moment. Instead, I felt like the last person on the dance floor when the music dies. The house lights were coming on, their florescent glare burning all magic from the world.

63

As soon as I got back to my hotel room, I wanted to leave it. The air was too dry. The ceiling too low. The bed too neatly made. I could smell housekeeping's cleaning products. I could barely distinguish the room from the innumerable other hotel rooms I'd spent a night or two in on mission after mission after mission. My past fanned out behind me like a deck of cards, each displaying an identical hotel room, and it was as if I could step into any of them and pick up where I'd left off without losing a beat.

My anticlimactic flower delivery made me worry I would *be* the climax. The French call orgasm *la petite mort*—"the little death"—and while I was bound up in tension that needed release, death, little or big, wasn't the kind of resolution I was looking for.

I had betrayed my nation, and my nation had betrayed me. Under Leia's duress, I had placed the world under Leia's duress, and now I could look forward to a life lived under ubiquitous and permanent duress. I don't mean to be bleak, but this was a bleak picture I'd helped paint, a bleak future I was ushering in.

A walk. I needed a walk to clear my head. To organize my fraying thoughts. I needed to get out of this damn room. Thunder pealed. Great. Of course it would start pouring as soon as I decided to go out for a stroll. Whatever. I grabbed my raincoat, pulled up the hood, stuffed my hands in the pockets, and–

There was something in the pocket of my raincoat: a neatly folded note. I scoured my memory. Yes, I'd last worn it the night of the typhoon, the night of the tearoom. Stomach clenching, I unfolded the note. It contained no message, only the address of a boutique hotel on a remote Greek island.

I told you: life is just one hotel room after another.

That's why I thought I knew what to expect.

I was wrong.

64

My eyes are locked on Caroline's. Struggling to keep the gun steady, I fire off question after question after question like a ball machine bombarding a sweating tennis player. Her answers do nothing to calm my trembling hands.

Liu was the crown jewel in Caroline's portfolio of agents. TSMC was rightfully wary of espionage, and it had taken years of relationship building to recruit him. Liu's importance to AIVD grew with the rising cachet of semiconductors, so you can imagine Caroline's outrage when she discovered that Barend had leveraged his high-level relationships to access Liu's file. She followed Barend to San Francisco, and then followed his contact, Lorenzo, from Analog to Miami. Tracking Lorenzo's comms, she saw he'd arranged to meet me, so she hired an on-demand assassin from Reap3r to take him out before he could sell me Liu's identity.

She returned to the Netherlands, ready to accuse Barend of treason, but he was at AIVD headquarters waiting for her, livid. He'd heard rumors that Leia was laying the foundation for a new intelligence paradigm, and that Holland could get in on the ground floor because of ASML's unique role in the semiconductor supply chain. Liu's identity had been part of the price of admission. Barend had used Lorenzo as a go-between to establish plausible deniability, and by having him killed on American soil, Caroline had also killed their chances of a covert partnership with Leia. Now, the Netherlands would have to muscle their way in to her scheme, which he ordered Caroline to do.

That's how she became my shadow, pickpocketing Phillip in a Threshold stairwell, showing up at key inflection points during my missions as a Resident at Large, siphoning off enough intel to ensure Holland could guarantee influence even if it was banished from Leia's inner circle. Meanwhile, Barend was determined to demonstrate that influence to Leia, which is why he reopened negotiations with China over access to ASML tools. He was flexing, and Leia had flexed back by sending me to drink his coffee, eat his appeltaart, and exert leverage.

Ultimately, Leia had still needed Liu to consummate her plan, but he had come cheap because AIVD didn't know enough to demand more.

Caroline draws new lines. She fills in gaps. She adds color and texture and depth and perspective. Of course, the whole picture goes beyond her answers, but I sketch missing sections with informed guesswork.

As I've mentioned, Leia always does things for more than one reason. In addition to giving Washington a new monopoly on power, her plan would effectively guarantee global monopolies for ASML and TSMC because our backdoor was built into their chips. So, of course, Leia had preemptively solicited buy-in from them.

My first impression of the Mindanao base was that it was too posh for government work, and I'm willing to bet Leia supplemented her black budget with clandestine investments from ASML and TSMC. Hell, I wouldn't be surprised if the pods' fancy tech was straight out of Threshold R&D.

The more I let my imagination roam, the more convinced I become of its speculations, which confirm Caroline's version of events. Everything had been too easy. If it hadn't been for Caroline's interventions, my missions would all have gone pretty much according to plan, which *never* happens, in espionage or in life. But if I was being deployed against covert partners, then the primary reason for my role had been to provide cover to their alliance. They couldn't risk collaborating openly, but they could afford to turn a blind eye, so I had played the spy, ferrying pawns and rooks and bishops between them so that Leia could orchestrate her Pax Silicon checkmate.

Games within games within games.

And the two of us at the center of them, here in this particular room, now at this particular moment upon which history turns.

There are crow's feet at the corners of Caroline's eyes. Her dark slash of hair is tangled. The light from the window turns half her face to gold—the other lies in shadow. She looks as tired as I feel.

The final piece falls into place.

"You're here to recruit me," I say, a statement of fact, not a question.

I've run out of those.

65

Caroline nods, not breaking eye contact.

"After Barend failed to buy his way into Operation Glass Ceiling, he decided to break in by having you recruit me," I say. Washington has pulled enough stunts like this one that even our friends invest in keeping an eye on us.

Caroline nods.

"I bet you even staged the attack by the church so we could save each other," I say. "A bonding exercise."

After a half-second's hesitation, Caroline nods.

You're almost certainly familiar with chess, but have you played go? It's a game that originated in China 2,500 years ago and is still played today. Each player starts out with a pile of small stones. You take turns placing them on the board, and the goal is to surround your opponent's stones, capturing them.

That's what spies do: we encircle each other.

If Caroline were to turn me, I'd be a huge asset for AIVD—by far the most influential double agent they'd ever run. I know what comes next. She'll offer me protection. She'll offer me money. She'll offer me a way out from under Leia's thumb. She'll offer me anything my heart desires that is within her nation's power to give. Therein lies her problem: I have no idea what I want anymore.

"That's what this is to you," I say, using the index finger of my free hand to draw a spiral between us, failing to keep the bitterness out of my voice. "A pitch."

Her sad frown is all the confirmation I need.

She opens her mouth to say something.

Closes it.

Opens it.

Closes it.

Swallows.

I have never seen Caroline at a loss for words.

She frowns again, but this time it's different—the sadness is gone, replaced by a bottomless intensity.

66

"**Do you trust me?**" Caroline demands. Her eyes are twin black holes sucking in the cosmos. I'm pointing the gun between them in a vain attempt to contain their dark energy.

"What?" My hands sweat against the grip. This is not going how it should be going. I'm the one holding the weapon. I'm supposed to be the one in charge. So why does it suddenly feel like I'm not?

"I said, 'Do you trust me?'" she repeats, glare unrelenting.

She should be answering *my* questions.

Fast as thought, her hands whip out and clap around the gun, fingers interlacing atop the barrel.

"*Do you trust me?*"

"Yes," I blurt out, which makes no sense at all and yet is somehow true.

She leans forward, eyes holding mine, and presses her forehead to the muzzle.

"Fire," she whispers.

"What? No. No—"

I try to jerk away, but her thumb snakes inside the trigger guard and forces my index finger.

I scream.

67

My abuela had X-ray vision.

Except she didn't see your ribs or vertebrae or femurs when she squinted at you. She saw deeper than that. She saw the skeletons in your closet. When she gazed out at the world, she did something almost nobody does. Most people see what they want to see. They see what they expect. They see what they fear. The world is a mirror reflecting what they already believe. My abuela was different. She saw the world for what it was.

Clairvoyants claim the supernatural ability to see the future or commune with the dead or perceive things beyond our standard senses. I first encountered the word "clairvoyant" when I was studying for a sixth-grade spelling bee. It's a compound of the French words *clair*, "clear", and *voir*, "to see." It was immediately obvious to me that the world was wrong to use it to describe psychics. This word existed to describe my abuela: she saw clearly.

It was her unerring vision that enabled her to survive the Cuban Revolution. To escape with her family to Florida. To build a new life from scratch on foreign soil. To shepherd her people through decades of turmoil. To raise a brood of grandchildren.

And then, on the eve of her 101st birthday, she died in her sleep.

All the brothers, sisters, parents, uncles, aunts, and many and varied cousins came together. We cried. We swapped stories. We ate. We sang. We drank. We argued. We hugged. We told jokes. We danced.

That was the last good night.

It wasn't that everything came crashing down all at once. This was a subtler apocalypse. It was a slow rot. A gradual corrosion. Because she'd always seen us for who we really were, we'd never learned to reveal ourselves to each other. So I hid my pain and, for the first time in my life, it actually worked. And I wasn't the only one. The family atomized. Each of us retreated into our own private grief. And when we began to emerge, we found that grief wasn't the only thing we could hide. At first, it was little things. A hard truth. An embarrassing mistake. A moment of vulnerability. But it didn't take long for them to get bigger. Within a few months, instead of being on the same team, we were playing games against each other.

Within a few years, the only thing we knew how to do was play games against each other.

How do you think I got good at espionage? When someone says you're a natural, it just means they don't realize how much practice you've had.

The day my abuela died was the last day I trusted someone. Our family relied on her vision and, in its absence, we were blind to each other. I haven't let myself be seen since.

68

Click.

Caroline's head does not explode.

Recoil does not jerk against my sweaty hands.

I do not lose this strange person I am unprepared to lose.

Eyes still locked on mine, she forces the trigger again, and this time I'm so unmoored I don't resist.

Click.

Click. Click. Click.

The gun isn't loaded.

Click. Click. Click.

THE FUCKING GUN ISN'T LOADED.

When she was holding the gun to my head, I was

completely at her mercy, which I believed put her at mine because I saw the safety was still on. When I was holding the gun to her head, safety off, I believed she was completely at my mercy, which put me at hers because she knew it wasn't loaded.

Click means the gun has been a prop from the beginning, that this was her plan the whole time. *Click* means this is play, not work. *Click* means this isn't an interrogation, but a conversation. *Click* means the drummer is striking up a new beat, and the band is rushing to catch up.

Caroline bites her lower lip.

My heart zigs. My heart zags. My heart leaps, drops, skips, and bursts. I could strangle her. I could kiss her. I could cry. I might very well go into cardiac arrest. The world may be bleak, but I am still in it. I am still here. And she is, too.

I can't help it. I start laughing. Huge gales of laughter roll through me, interspersed with fits of giggles. And then she starts laughing too and we're both setting each other off and gasping for air and laughing and laughing and laughing until tears are rolling down our faces and stitches are forming in our sides and the gun falls to the floor, forgotten, and something broken is inexplicably whole.

69

The laughter finally recedes, leaving us spreadeagled on the carpet. I stare up at the ceiling, tracing the complex topography of white plaster. Gulls harass each other somewhere out over the harbor. The afternoon light filtering in through the fluttering curtains grows warmer, richer, suffusing the room with an amber glow.

We lie in comfortable silence for a long time. I can't remember when I last felt genuinely at ease, a foreign emotion to someone with my vocation. It buoys me, and, in doing so, loosens something inside me, just as the right stretch can sometimes relieve a muscle you didn't realize was tight.

Caroline begins to speak.

She tells me about growing up in The Hague. She tells me about joining AIVD. She tells me which of her digital ghosts are signal and which are noise.

She tells me how deeply she loves the Netherlands, and why. The cosmopolitan culture. The unapologetic frankness. The herring. The bicycles. The feeling of being a tiny country determined to play a large role in a giant world.

She tells me how she sometimes hates the Netherlands. How much bullshit she had to suffer because her grandfather was Indonesian. How many people she'd had to kill to cover up the Shell contractor's role in the Baluchi pogrom. How the Dutch royal family uses the government to protect its wealth. How, with their blessing, Barend is quietly exploiting AIVD to fulfill his lifelong dream of restoring the Dutch Empire—a prospect that disgusts her.

She tells me how frustrated she is by the very fact that's she's an *agent*, by definition someone else's tool, how badly she wants to make decisions instead of execute them. She tells me how much fun she had that night on the Tibetan Plateau. She tells me how the smell of jasmine after an evening rain moves her in a way she can't explain. She tells me that she doesn't know what she wants anymore, either. She tells me more than I ever could have guessed, more than I ever could have asked. She tells me things I identify with. She tells me things that change what I identify with.

And then, she's done.

The silence returns, but it's different this time: full, pregnant, expectant. It's a magnetic silence. A silence asking to be filled.

70

I fill it.

I tell Caroline everything I had strategically withheld during the interrogation. I add the missing pieces. I connect the dots. I tell her how bad the coffee is in the Mindanao base, that it doesn't bear comparison to her cortados. I tell her how I taught Samantha salsa while she was teaching me violence. I tell her about Bisrat's wizardry. I tell her about how much I resent my affection for Jerry. I tell her how much I enjoyed chatting with Liu in the TSMC cafeteria. I tell her how I bullied Phillip in the shadow of the Burghers of Calais. I tell her about Barend's appeltaart. I tell her about the surreal midnight rendezvous with Ae-cha on the Sea of Japan. I tell her about the innocent people I murdered. I tell her about Leia's dreams, and the trap she set for me.

And I don't stop there. Giddy with the risk of it, I tell her what I think. I tell her what I feel. It helps that we're not making eye contact, that I can follow the vertiginous peaks and valleys of plaster and let my voice go where it wills. I tell her about my once grand ambitions, which now seem so very petty. I tell her how little I have to lose, how espionage slowly eroded my sense of connection, how working in the shadows transformed me into a shadow, how empty and brittle my life has become.

I tell her about my abuela. I tell her how much the freedom we found in America meant to my family, how I had started down this path to safeguard that freedom, only to find myself projecting power instead, a weapon in service to hegemony. I tell her how sad it makes me to see my nation lead by force instead of example, how it makes me question whether ideals I once held were little more than naïveté, how sick I am of it all, how every path leads back to the center of the labyrinth. I tell her things I've never told anyone else. I tell her things I won't even tell you. I tell her that I want to let myself be seen again, and fuck the consequences.

When I finally reach the end, my heart is light and my throat is raw.

71

Silence washes over us a third time.

I roll onto my side.

Caroline rolls to face me.

Only two feet of carpet separate us.

I feel more like a kid than I ever did as a kid.

She bites her lip.

I reach up and my hand brushes against the gun, but I push it aside and pull the briefcase out from under the bed. Popping it open, I carefully remove a small morning-glory pod from the secret compartment. I took the cutting as insurance while preparing the boutonnière. The engineered DNA in these cells contains the recipe for Leia's exploit. All we need to do is plant a seed.

I wink.
She rolls her eyes.

72

I slip into my boat shoes, and we walk down to the shore. The path from the hotel descends through a narrow cleft in the bluff, stratified rock rising steeply up on either side of rough stone steps. I run my fingertips along the patterns, imagining the geological violence in which they formed.

When we step out onto the sand, the world opens up around us. A crescent beach tucked into rugged cliffs. Waves tumbling up and hissing back into the deep. The sun a scarlet ember on the horizon, igniting cloud fortresses rising high into a lapis sky.

We kick off our shoes and let the surf wash over our ankles.

This would be a great location to program into one of the Mindanao pods. I remember Leia staring down at me from her perch on a Joshua Tree boulder, cold stars blazing above us.

What if I don't want to turn the world into your puppet show?

What you want has nothing to do with it.

I realize that despite what she'd done, despite what she'd made me do, despite the fact that she's from California, I don't hate Leia. It's just that by dreaming of world domination, she dreams too small.

As the sun drops below the horizon and color drains from the world, something stirs inside me, something unfamiliar, something new. I don't rush it. I let it find its form. I let the words find me.

Finally, I say, "What if we switch things up? Not as a game or a front, but for real. What if we choose a different path? What if we change?"

"What do you mean?" asks Caroline.

"I don't know," I say. "But I want to find out."

Her lips quirk into a puzzled half-smile.

And then there is a flash and a roar and we are slammed to the sand and I am trying to catch my breath and smoke is pouring from our hotel—dark billows lit by flame—and debris is tumbling down the cliff face and I'm looking over at Caroline to see if she's OK and see her looking over at me and I can't tell if I'm injured through the avalanche of adrenaline but I don't *think* I'm hurt and I don't see any blood on Caroline and she's breathing and I'm breathing—that's right, I need to remember to breathe—and we push ourselves to our feet and our ears are ringing and we stare up at the gaping, glowing hole where our suite used to be and Caroline, gasping, says, "Drone strike."

And those two words close a circuit in my brain and I'm back on Mindanao and Samantha is kicking my ass for the seven-hundred-and-fifty-sixth time and, with her knee in my chest and her knife at my throat, I politely request that if she's ever ordered to kill me, she does so with a drone strike so I don't see it coming.

I can't help it, I burst out laughing.

"We don't have time for you to go into shock," says Caroline. "My money's on Leia tying up loose ends now that she has what she wants."

"Oh, Leia definitely ordered the hit," I say. "But the funny thing about orders is that people still have to choose to follow them."

I look up and blow a kiss to the darkening sky where I know the Residents must have surveillance drones and satellites staring down at us. They've been watching the whole time, and if Samantha waited until we left the hotel to blow up the suite, that means Bisrat will be wiping our exit, and my blown kiss, from the record. A parting gift to a fellow traveler, a gift to spite Leia and her Beltway colleagues with their endless machinations, the priceless gift of presumed death.

I take Caroline's hand, and run.

73

We're running still.

We stole a small sailboat, disabled the GPS, and voyaged to a neighboring island, where I was grateful not to encounter giant Cyclopes like Odysseus did when he crossed this very sea, although you could make a case for Caroline being my Circe, and vice versa. From there, we took a series of public ferries to the mainland and then traveled overland to Istanbul, which is a magnificent city to lose yourself in. Then off to Tunis, and Cape Town, and Hobart, and Auckland, and Lima, and Oaxaca, and Reykjavik, and on and on and on.

Many writers outline stories with extraordinary precision before they embark on a draft. They make detailed plans, and then execute them. That is not how Caroline and I are writing the story of what has become our shared life, which I'm documenting here so you'll know the truth even if we're discovered. Instead, we are writing it sentence by sentence, page by page, chapter by chapter, discovering the story as we go, every decision subject to revision.

We invented new identities for ourselves, made new friends, listened to new music, experimented with new ways of living. We comforted each other on the nights when one of us woke up screaming, which was most nights. I taught her to dance. She taught me to cook. We channeled Samantha to keep us safe, we channeled Bisrat to keep us hidden, and we channeled Jerry to keep us whole.

In spy movies, the protagonist is always on the verge of retirement, but can never truly escape. We have made it our mission to prove that trope wrong. We raised a brood of our own, and while we didn't send our kids to charter school, we did build an off-grid insulated yurt in Kamchatka for whenever we really need to blow off some steam.

To support our family—and to satisfy our intrigue addiction—we design board games that we sell pseudonymously on Kickstarter. They are astonishingly successful. I think I know why. Our fans don't realize it, but each of our games is based on one of our clandestine operations. Players simulate every possible variation of what we've lived though, grappling with veiled versions of Leia, Barend, Lorenzo, Phillip, Ae-cha, Liu, and all the other ghosts that haunt us.

You've probably played one, but you might not realize

that every board game we design is collaborative. You don't play against each other. You play with each other against the game. Jerry loves them. I'm not joking. I checked. He's bought copies of every single one of our games for each of his seven grandchildren. There's no way for him to know who created the games or what they're really about, but I swear he's worked it out. It's all too easy to imagine him dropping nuggets like, "Over the long run, all games are collaborative."

Fucking Jerry.

Oh, and everywhere we go, we plant morning glories. Their vines crawl up Moroccan walls. Their roots tap Cambodian soil. Their leaves shade Brazilian pergolas. Their blossoms delight Mongolian toddlers. Butterflies drink their nectar, teenagers pick them for crushes, and, when they're in full bloom, everyone posts pics of them on Instagram, although nobody suspects the secret they carry in their genes.

Espionage is all about constructing artificial relationships. You figure out what makes people tick and then you rearrange the clockwork. The problem is that the better you get at it, the more your life becomes a facsimile. You have sources, but no friends. You have agents, but no lovers. You have colleagues, but no family. You are a master horologist living inside a mechanical watch.

Now, whenever I find myself falling into that kind of thinking, I feel the barrel of the gun twist into my forehead. I heft its grip in memory's sweaty palm.

Do you trust me?

Click.

The empty chamber was a proposal, an invitation to become someone new, to change that which I had never dared risk, to grow together, two indomitable weeds sharing the same patch of rocky soil, the same bittersweet rain, the same beloved, infernal sun.

74

You thought that was the end, right? It could have been, but like I told you at the beginning, this is my story, and I'm sticking to it, and if you've stuck with me this long, then you know that I'm the kind of guy who likes to run my mouth, even when it gets me into trouble. So let's get into a little more trouble before we go our separate ways.

If you look directly at Medusa, you turn to stone. The problems in your life are Medusas. They're too big, too complicated, too interconnected. When you appraise them, it feels like nothing you can do will make a difference, so you do nothing. You turn to stone.

But if you look at Medusa's reflection in a mirrored shield, you can safely glimpse her flared wings and writhing snakes, you can see how to approach her and where to swing your sword. Art is just such a mirrored shield. By reflecting the world, it can reveal how to change it.

In retrospect, our mutual interrogation in that hotel room was a kind of performance art. Caroline and I could see in each other's stories what we couldn't see when looking directly at the world. We could see an approach, and where to swing our sword.

We realized that doing the right thing was more important than following orders. We were patriots, once. We outsourced our principles to our respective nations and suffered the consequences. Now, we were ourselves sovereign, and willing to suffer the consequences. Sacrifice for your conscience, not your country, because moral societies emerge from moral citizens. Or, you know, do whatever the fuck you want, but recognize that for better and for worse, change starts with each of us.

Leia established her Pax Silicon. Washington got its second American Century. We waited patiently during those years of relative peace and stability. We knew what was coming. My abuela ensured all us cousins studied the history of the Roman Empire beat by beat. Power is a stiff drink, and it didn't take long for America to revert to nasty drunk. As soon as the United States began abusing its reclaimed status as hegemon, "necessary tragedies" multiplying, we printed out tens of thousands of copies of the decryption key along with morning-glory geotags and snail-mailed them to every graduate of every computer-science program on the planet.

We shattered Operation Glass Ceiling with the flower from which it had bloomed. Not to secure victory for ourselves or defeat our opponents—although Leia was ruined—but to keep the game alive. To keep playing. You know me. I'm all about the *dance*. And when the dance is as big and dumb and messy and beautiful as human civilization, I want to keep the party going.

Will it work? Will we succeed in keeping the game alive a while longer? Who knows? If you know something's going to work, it's not worth working on. It requires no courage. It requires no faith. It requires no skin in the game. Whether you're a spy or a teacher or a spouse or a painter or an abuela or an astronaut or a monk or a barista or a board-game designer, the bits that matter are the bits you *make* matter by putting yourself on the line for them. The unknown is the foundry where you forge your chips. Everything important is uncertain. Sitting with the discomfort of that uncertainty is the hard part, the wedge that can move the world.

Oh, and it's none of your damn business, but yes, Caroline and I continue to have every inch of (frequently flushed) skin in our own private game. It's not perfect. Nothing ever is. There's just life—and whether you choose to share it—until there isn't. That's where the courage and faith come in. To make a life together was to be forever putting ourselves at each other's mercy, chamber loaded, safety off.

THE END

WRITING *FOUNDRY*

Foundry began with a dream.

I woke up in the middle of the night with no memory of the dream's larger context, but a single remnant image hanging in my mind, my heart foundering in its emotional wake. Rolling over, I made a quick note, and then fell back asleep.

The next morning, I read the note:

It wasn't that she was holding a gun to my head. It was that I could see the safety was still on. She thought I was completely at her mercy, which was what put her at mine.

Curtains billowed in my imagination and, beyond them, I glimpsed a fading dreamscape of bright blue domes, whitewashed walls, turquoise sea. I wanted to know who these people were, what they cared about, where they came from, why they were at odds, and how they had arrived at this paradoxical crux. It wasn't an intellectual desire so much as an ache—how a detective might yearn to close a particularly puzzling case.

A thought arrived, unbidden: that's the opening line of a novel. The only way to answer my questions would be to write it. So I transcribed the note, and then wrote the next sentence, and then the next, and then the one after that. Sentences became paragraphs, paragraphs became chapters, and the chapters kept multiplying until I found my way back to that room with Adrian and Caroline and together we reached an ending.

I usually write with a plan. The plans vary in scope and detail, but I have an idea of where I'm going in a particular story. Plans can be extremely helpful. Instead of deciding between destinations, I can focus on figuring out the best way to get there. But the cleverer the plan, the more painful it is when it breaks. Writing other novels, I'd realize halfway through that my plan didn't work anymore, and that realization would spark a creative crisis. I would spend weeks or months struggling to find a solution—gaming out possibilities, soliciting advice from friends, rearranging narrative variables. Often, it felt impossible, like I might need to give up entirely and archive the manuscript. Eventually, I manage to find a new way forward, but not without a lot of angst.

Foundry was different. I was writing the story line-by-line. I had no plan. This meant that I was in a *permanent* creative crisis. I didn't know where we were going. I discovered what happened next alongside the reader.

Drafting the manuscript was a slow dance with the unknown. Again and again, it felt impossible. Without a plan, I was constantly improvising, rereading that opening line thousands of times, using the material that had accrued on the previous page to draft the next page. Simultaneously, without a plan, I had no emotional investment in the plan working out. There were no sunk costs. No attachments. No angst. I was free to experiment, to play. It was exhilarating and terrifying and tremendous fun.

Writing *Foundry* changed my relationship with uncertainty. Unlike Adrian, I'm a terrible dancer, but I know enough to understand that you don't control your partner, you follow each others' cues. Dancing with the unknown was an exercise in paying ever closer attention to what was on the page, letting the story reveal itself, summoning the courage to say "I don't know" in order to create the space for knowledge to arrive.

"I don't know" is fundamental to how fiction works. Leave professed certainty to the aspiring influencers. Novels are vehicles for wondering what if, for seeking other points of view, for celebrating complexity, for exploring questions without easy answers, for voyaging elsewhere. And, every once in a while, when you encounter the right story at the right time, you return from that voyage changed, armed with new ways of seeing.

Thanks for reading,
Eliot

P.S. The best way to follow my writing is to subscribe to my newsletter at www.eliotpeper.com

THANKS

To Brad Feld and Amy Batchelor for providing the generous grant that made *Foundry* possible.

To Kevin Barrett Kane for the beautiful cover and interior design.

To Peter Nowell for the inspiring concept art.

To Pamela Lorence for directing and producing the audiobook.

To Tim Erickson and Amanda Rutter for the salutary edits.

To Josh Anon, Hannu Rajaniemi, and Lucas Carlson for the advice on early drafts.

To John Carmack, Chris Miller, Sha Rabii, Harshit Khaitan, Rob Shearer, Marco Brambilla, Pankaj Goel, Azeem

Azhar, Dave Goldblatt, Kwame Boateng, T.H. Schee, Marija Gavrilov, Jake Chapman, Danny Crichton, and Ryan McIntyre for teaching me about semiconductors.

To Seth Godin, Robin Sloan, Kim Stanley Robinson, and Malka Older for the encouragement.

To my paid newsletter subscribers who invest in my writing so I can do more of it.

To Drea, Ash, and Claire for embarking on this journey together and sticking with it every step of the way.

And to you, dear reader, for bringing *Foundry* to life in the theater of your mind.

ABOUT THE AUTHOR

Eliot Peper is the author of eleven novels,
including *Bandwidth*, *Veil*, *Cumulus*, and *Reap3r*.
He also consults on special projects and helps founders
build technology businesses. The best way to follow
his writing is to subscribe to his newsletter.

WWW.ELIOTPEPER.COM

Printed in the USA
CPSIA information can be obtained
at www.ICGtesting.com
LVHW092314271223
767605LV00018B/62/J